The

It's not every day the cat catches a mouse and puts it in your boot. It's not every day the cuckoo clock pinches your breakfast sausage. It's not every day the dog eats your comic and blows a fuse.

To George and Cynthia, in fact, stuck out on the Yorkshire Moors with a totally mad professor and a huge (not to say tiny) problem, these little things just about put the tin lid on it. Something's got to happen, and it's got to happen *NOW!*

Well it does. Before they know exactly what's hit them, they're in the thick of an absolutely lunatic adventure, involving spies, dangerous inventions, two peculiar boys called Jugears and Mophead, and a set of stolen parents. Before much longer they've got themselves into a right old mess.

The Size Spies is very exciting, and a lot of fun. But watch out – it could happen to you!

Jan Needle

The Size Spies

Illustrated by
Roy Bentley

Lions

First published 1979
by André Deutsch Limited
First published in Lions 1980
Sixth impression July 1987

Lions is an imprint of
the Children's Division, part of
the Collins Publishing Group,
8 Grafton Street, London W1X 3LA

Made and printed in Great Britain by
William Collins Sons & Co. Ltd, Glasgow

Ode to a title – now sadly no more

'I've got a novel for you, Mrs Royds,' I said.
To Pam, the children's editor of this here
publishing house.
'It's called The Sly Size Spies Saga.
Rather good that, eh? It's a
tongue-twister, give the kids a laugh.'
'Cor, stone me,' she replied. 'Sply Slies Pies What, old chum?
Imagine comin' aht with that to some pore
bookshop girl. You must be orf your rocker.'
(She's a Londoner, see, like Polly, her assistant.)
'Change it.'
She's the boss, I'm the author.
So I changed it.

Whatever it's called, it's still for
Margaret and Jimmy,
Guy and Kit,
and Robbie.

Contents

One of Those Days

Cynthia and George realised it was going to be that sort of a day from the very start. They woke up early because the wind howling across the Yorkshire Moors was shaking the window frames of the old house and every now and again a spatter of rain rattled against the panes like machine-gun bullets. It was cold in the bedroom and for a while they lay with just their noses sticking out, watching the four jets of vapour rising towards the ceiling as they breathed.

'You know, George,' said Cynthia. 'If it rains today it'll be the sixteenth day on the trot. I'm fed up with it.'

'Yes,' said George.

'It's all very well living out here, miles from anywhere,

and everybody saying how lucky we are, but sometimes I wonder. You know.'

'Yes,' said George.

'All right, so the house is old, and it's meant to be beautiful, and all that sort of a thing. But just look at that water dripping into the bowl. The place leaks like anything. And if those window frames get much shakier they'll drop straight out.'

George pulled himself up on to one elbow to look at the water dripping from the ceiling. Every other drop missed the bowl and fell onto the bare floor because of the wind zipping through the room.

'Draughty too,' he said.

Cynthia would have gone on moaning, but it was her turn to get breakfast, which meant it was George's turn to pump up the water.

'Come on,' she said. 'I suppose we'd better get up.'

As George slipped his foot into his boot he felt something squidgy with his toes. He wiggled them about, trying to work out what it was. Then he sat on the bed, turned the boot upside-down, and shook. A dead mouse fell on to his hand. He gave a shout of surprise. The mouse flew into the air.

'That cat! That stupid cat! It's never worked properly! It *knows* it's meant to put them outside!'

Cynthia laughed.

'Good old Viva,' she said. 'She might be unreliable, but she's not a bad mouser.'

'Well there's plenty for her to practise on,' George said grumpily. 'Go on then, Cynth. Get the breakfast on.'

When George came back into the kitchen from drawing the water Cynthia had a puzzled look on her face.

'You know, George, I don't like the sound of that. Listen.'

'What to?' said George, wiping the dewdrop off the end of his nose with his sleeve. 'All I can hear is the rotten wind. It's blowing a gale out there.'

'Not the wind, daftie. The breakfast machine.'

He cocked his head on one side to listen. Something did seem to be different. A kind of clanking noise.

'Did you put the fat in?' he asked. 'Sounds . . . you know, sort of dry.'

'Course I did, stupid. I have cooked breakfast before! I put in one knob of fat, one sausage, one egg . . . '

'What are you talking about?' said George. '*One* sausage? *One* egg? There's three of us!'

'Don't care if there's ten of us,' said Cynthia. 'That's all we've got left. I don't know what the Prof's thinking of. There's nothing at all in the cupboard. It's empty.'

She broke off with a shriek. Suddenly the machine, which was square, and squat, and covered with funny pipes and knobs, started to shake about on its little short legs.

'Turn it off,' George shouted. 'Get that switch! Quick!'

Too late. With a loud cough the machine shot the sausage out. They watched in amazement as it flew across the kitchen, which was low with blackened old beams. The sausage reached the cuckoo clock at exactly ten to eight. But the cuckoo – designed by the Prof – darted out, speared it on its beak, and disappeared. Ten minutes later, instead of eight clear, loud 'cuckoos', all they got was one 'cuck', one strangled gurgle, and a loud burp.

'You see,' said Cynthia in disgust. 'Even the cuckoo's starving!'

The fried egg chose a different direction. It went sailing towards the door to the living room. Which opened, of course, at just the right moment.

'Ah,' said the Prof. 'Good m—'

Even the sight of his surprised face, with yolk dribbling off his chin into his waistcoat neck, didn't cheer up Cynthia. She flounced down into a chair pouting.

'I'm fed up with this house,' she said. 'Nothing ever works, and it's all your fault. *Now* what are we going to do for breakfast?'

Naturally enough the Prof didn't answer. He was too busy eating the egg off his beard and moustache. All he seemed able to say was 'Mmm', and 'Very nice', and 'Well cooked, my dear'.

Just to put the tin lid on it, just to prove that it was going to be one of those days, the Snark came in just then, with what was left of the paper and Cynthia's comic. Unlike Viva, the Snark was usually very reliable indeed. Although he had to run eight miles there and eight miles back every morning to the paper shop in the village, he usually managed it without any bother at all. But today, of all days (because it was comic day) he seemed to have gone wrong. The papers hanging down from each side of his mouth were soggy, and tattered, and muddy, and *completely* unreadable.

'Snark!' shouted Cynthia. 'What *have* you done! You *bad* dog!'

The Prof tutted.

'Oh dear, oh dear. How annoying. One of his transistors must be on the blink.'

He made a clicking noise with his mouth. The Snark, dropping the drippy mess of chewed paper, trotted happily over to him. The Prof leaned down, as if to scratch him behind the ear. There was a click.

'There,' said the Prof, lifting the rigid dog onto the kitchen table. 'I'll have a look at him after breakfast.'

'You and your silly pets,' said Cynthia. 'Look at my comic. A real dog wouldn't do a thing like that.'

A bit later, as they shared a slice of bread and dripping, the Prof came out with some news that made all the other things seem like a joke. Some really awful news.

'Had a bad morning, have you, Cynthia?' he asked kindly. 'I'm very sorry to hear that, my dear, very sorry.'

'That's all right, Prof,' said Cynthia. 'I think it's the weather really. Sometimes the moors do get a bit much, you must admit. And then there being no food in. It's very bad of you to let us run out.'

The Prof shook his head sadly.

'It's not a case of running out, my dear,' he said. 'I'm afraid that's it. That's the last of the food.'

'What do you mean?' asked Cynthia. 'No more food? But how are we going to live?'

'You can't live without food, you know,' said George. 'Even a scientist should know that much, Prof! And what about the parents, anyway?'

The Prof took a swig of tea from his china mug.

'Oh dear, George,' he said. 'You've touched on a raw spot, I'm afraid. I wanted to have a talk with you children about it. The fact is, you see, I've run out. The cupboard is bare. The coffers are empty. In short, my dear – we're flat broke.'

Cynthia was horrified.

'If we haven't got enough to buy food,' she said, 'what about Mum and Dad?'

'Exactly,' said the Prof.

'What will they say?' asked Cynthia.

'I wonder,' said the Prof.

'More to the point,' added George, who was always very practical, 'what are we going to do about it?'

'Aah,' said the Prof. 'That, as they say, is the question.'

The children were full of ideas, but the Prof shot them down one by one. Taking the lemonade bottles back might buy them breakfast, and even dinner (there were always a lot around the house because it was so far to the shop and their memories were bad). But it would not, he said, help the parents. And George's idea of raiding the piggy bank was no good either, he said. Even if they could get into it, what would they find? Not much, he reckoned. As for having a jumble sale (Cynthia's plan) it was out of the question. When had anyone last walked past the house?

'Anyway,' he said gently. 'I don't think you quite understand what I'm talking about. I'm not talking about pocket-money, you know. I've nothing. For food, for coal, for heat, for light. Not a penny. It's very very serious.'

George pondered.

'And how much do you need?' he asked. 'You know, for everything? Plus the parents, of course.'

The Prof thought for a full two minutes.

'At least ten thousand,' he said. 'At least.'

'POUNDS!' shrieked Cynthia.

'Phew!' said George. 'That's *awful*!'

In the end, after a lot more talking, they decided to ask the Thinks Computer. Like a lot of the Prof's inventions it was not perfect, but when it came to working things out it was usually better than its inventor. Or the two children. Or all three put together. Its main problem was that it thought in rhyme – very bad rhyme. The Prof said it would be quite easy to put right if he had enough money, but he never did. And at the moment, there were far more important things to spend it on anyway.

The Thinks Computer sat in the living room, about

where the television would be in a normal house, humming softly to itself. Red and blue lights flickered across its front, and Viva was snoring gently on its warm, polished dome. When the Prof had typed out the question and fed it into the proper slot, the lights flickered faster, the hum took on a higher pitch, and the unreliable cat leapt to the floor with a squawk. That dome got hot!

The question obviously wasn't a very hard one for a computer to answer. For it was only about four and a quarter minutes later that the humming changed pitch and the 'Ready to Inform' light flashed on. The Prof pressed the 'Clear' button and they pinned back their ears.

The machine cleared its throat (or at least, that's what it sounded like) then spoke in a strange and scratchy voice:

> It's very early in the day to be
> disturbed by you
> A little more consideration in future
> wouldn't do
> You any harm with me, in fact, I'd
> work a whole lot better –
> But never mind I'll let you off
> Yes off I'm going to letyer.
>
> Call that a problem anyway? The
> answer's crystal clear
> If you want loot to put things right
> to London you must steer.
> Go to the Government, my friend, put there
> your case before 'em.
> They know your name, they know your fame,
> I'm sure they won't ignore 'em.
>
> There's your advice, but one thing more
> Before you leave this add-ress.
> If you'd thought more a lot before,
> You'd not be in this sad mess.

P.S. In case you muck things up
When you're away from home,
Make sure my flexing arm is clear
And near enough the phone.

When they got into the kitchen again, well out of earshot, Cynthia almost spat!

'Holier than thou, smug, self-satisfied, self-important tin horror,' she said. 'It's too big for its boots by half. And that's a fact!'

'Yes,' said George. 'But we've got a problem. A bad one. And we've *got* to solve it. It may be smug, but at least it can think. I suppose we ought to be grateful.'

CHAPTER TWO

Feeding the Parents

It didn't take them long to decide who should tell the parents the bad news. Cynthia was very good with parents, much better than George, although she did tend to get her name in the punishment book more often. As she prepared their breakfast, they discussed exactly what they should be told.

'Well,' said George, practically, 'I vote we tell them everything. Just come out with it and see what they say.'

Cynthia sniffed.

'I like your style I must say,' she said. 'What do you mean *we* tell them everything? You'll be miles away, pretending to clean the stove or something. I'm the one who's going to get it in the neck.'

'You know what I mean, Cleverclogs,' George replied. 'Don't be such a smart alec. Just come out and say it to them.'

The Prof waved his teaspoon at them both.

'Now don't start bickering, children, don't start bickering. Not today of all days when we've a lot to do.'

'Huh!' said Cynthia nastily. 'All you're doing is drinking tea. At the very least you could have a look at poor Snark. You know he hates being switched off.'

'Yes, dear, yes, dear. But try not to be so impolite, it does upset me.'

'Well. If we went to school like ordinary children they'd teach us manners. It's hardly our fault, now, is it?'

George knew that this sort of argument could go on

indefinitely when Cynthia was in one of her moods. He tried to be sensible.

'Look, Cynth,' he said, 'don't bring all that up now. I know what you mean about being normal; I'd like to be, too, sometimes, especially stuck out here in weather like this. But just think – if we were, we wouldn't be bowling off to London, now would we?'

Cynthia was still prepared to argue, but you could tell by her voice that her temper had improved.

'Neither would I have to go and tell Mum and Dad the bad news.' She gave a short laugh. 'Bet you tuppence I get my name in the book!'

From somewhere, way at the back of the house, came the sudden and shockingly loud sound of a brass band.

'Oh cripes,' said George. 'Hail Smiling Morn! He's off early today. Hurry up, Cynthia, or you'll get in every page. He must be waiting for his breakfast.'

Cynthia started to skip about, getting everything ready.

'Get me some ice, George, quick. Now where's the tray? Oh Prof, pass me that little teapot.'

When George had broken some ice away from the fridge and crushed it up very small, Cynthia added a spoonful to the things on her tray and headed for the door. The Prof held it open for her with an anxious smile.

'Now be careful what you say, dear child. Be diplomatic. We don't want him to bump up the volume, do we?'

With the kitchen door open the sound of the brass band was amazing. They certainly didn't want him to bump up the volume!

The house on the Yorkshire Moors was stone, and very old, and very big. It rambled. Over the centuries bits had been added on here and there, as if at random. It sometimes seemed that the people who had owned it through the years must have occasionally – or even quite often! – gone up to the rise of the moor above the house, looked down at the higgledy-piggledy straggle, and said to themselves: 'Hhmm.

Let's add a bit on there,' or 'Another lump sticking out of that corner would look a treat, I reckon.' Maybe in the old days there was little else to keep you amused on the Yorkshire Moors.

From a cleaning point of view, or from heating, or keeping out the damp, or holding down the mice, the house was a disaster. But in one very important respect it was very useful indeed. As Cynthia walked slowly through the cold, bare rooms, along the cobwebby passages and through the creaking, broken-panelled doors, she blessed its very size. For as she approached the room which was absolutely the farthest possible from the bit she, George and the Prof lived in, the noise of Hail Smiling Morn became truly deafening.

The trouble was Father.

Before the accident, which had happened all too long ago, Father, like the Prof, had been an inventor. He'd invented different sorts of things from the Prof, and he'd also been an amateur nuclear physicist of some note. But his real love in life (apart from Mother, of course, and Oldham Breweries bitter) had been brass band music. In fact, just before the fatal day, he'd achieved an incredible breakthrough. He had perfected the world's first and only one-man twenty-six piece brass band.

Now this might not sound too difficult to anyone who knows nothing about brass bands. But don't forget – the one-man sound included a soprano cornet, a repiano cornet, eight other cornets and a flugelhorn, two euphoniums, three trombones, four basses (two E-flat and two B-flat), a solo horn – well, the list is very long. Twenty six long in fact. And Father had compressed this all into one instrument, which looked rather like an oversized cornet expecting quins. When he put it to his lips and blew, out came:

Hail Smiling Morn!

The problem was, that whatever time of day it was, or sometimes even night, to Father's one-man twenty-six

piece brass band it was always Smiling Morn. And he
Hailed it.

Even worse, was that as he worked on the invention to
perfect it, after the accident, he didn't aim towards greater
variety, he aimed towards greater volume. Hail Smiling
Morn got louder and louder and louder and louder. Until
it was louder, perhaps, than a real, twenty-six man twenty-
six piece brass band. And much as the children and the
Prof loved the parents, with the best will in the world they
couldn't stand it. So they moved them slowly farther and
farther away from the kitchen and the living room, until at
last they were stuck out here, at the farthest possible point
And still the bass trombone sometimes shook the china in
the Welsh dresser.

Cynthia waited almost patiently until the last notes died
away before thrusting the door quickly open and nipping
in. Before Father got a chance to start again she shouted:
'Come on, you two! Grub up! Less of the noise now!'

Her mother's voice came back from out of the corner,
thin and a bit cross: 'Now now, Cynthia, how many times
do I have to tell you not to speak to your parents like that?
Your manners get worse every day.'

'Sorry, Mum,' said Cynthia cheerfully. She certainly
didn't want to start an argument today; not with the news
she had to break. 'What I meant to say was "Here's
breakfast, parents dear. Did you sleep well and is there
anything I can get for you please?" '

Father's voice: 'And there's no need to be cheeky,
either.'

Blimey, thought Cynthia, there's no pleasing some
people.

She put down the little tray on a cleanish table and went
into the farthest corner of the room. There, on top of a big
packing case, was the parents' house. She unclipped the
front gently, so as not to rock it, and took it off, so that she
could see into every room.

It was a doll's house really, of the good old-fashioned

Victorian sort. It had been Mother's when she was a little girl, and her mother's before her, so it was appropriate in a way that she should live in it now. After the accident the Prof had dug it out of the loft and cleaned it up. He'd also made some additions and improvements. Now it had everything a modern house could ask. Central heating, good plumbing, and fitted wardrobes in the main bedroom. It also had a big carrying handle on the roof, but that wasn't needed anymore, because there was no further place the house could be carried to.

Mother was still in bed, with her saggy ice-bag tied on to her head with a ribbon. Father was sitting at the kitchen table, in his pyjamas. The one-man twenty-six piece brass band device was on the table in front of him. Cynthia had an urge to grab it and crush it underfoot, but she fought it down. After all, it wasn't the parents' fault that all this had happened to them. It was no wonder, really, that they were so difficult to live with, considering.

She didn't say anything about the cash trouble while she sorted out the breakfast things. She told them how the Snark had chewed up her comic, which made Dad laugh, and she mentioned the flying sausage and egg, which made even Mother smile. But mainly she just wittered on about nothing in particular while they ate their tiny platters of cereal, followed by toast and Bovril. (Even with the cupboard bare finding enough for the parents was no trouble.)

When they'd finished eating she emptied the water out of Mother's ice-bag and refilled it with the ice George had crushed. As usual the fresh ice, along with a good breakfast, made Mother feel a lot better. If only Father had invented something quieter, thought Cynthia, none of it would have been necessary anyway. Ah well.

But at last she could put it off no longer. Dad, in fact, asked her directly what they were all planning to do today. All Cynthia's carefully thought out sentences went clean from her memory. She blurted out: 'We're going to London. We've got to!'

A stony silence.

'Going to London? Whatever are you talking about, my lass?'

Mother said: 'Really, Cynthia! This is just too bad! Gadding about all over the place when your father and I are stuck here like this! The very idea!'

Father: 'Well just tell the Prof that he can forget the whole thing. We've been in this state quite long enough. If he had an ounce of decency he'd be in that inventing room twenty four hours a day finding a way to get us back to normal. No consideration! None at all!'

Mother: 'Nobody cares for us! Nobody cares a jot! You're a dreadful selfish girl with an awful selfish brother and the Prof is just the giddy limit!'

This was too much for Cynthia. She stamped her foot and bellowed.

'You silly pair of parents! How dare you think that!

That's why we've got to go to London. The Prof's run out of money helping you, and if we don't get some more he'll never finish the deshrinker. You'll stay little for ever! And I don't think I care!'

Then she said something really terrible, all things considered. She shouted: 'It's about time you GREW UP!'

CHAPTER THREE

Getting to London

Cynthia was still in tears when she got back to the kitchen. George poured her a cup of tea with an extra spoonful of sugar. The Prof, bent over the Snark with a long screwdriver in his hand, pretended not to notice.

'Have a hard time did you, Cynth?' George asked as she gulped down the strong sweet tea. 'Did you get put in the book?'

Cynthia sniffed a few times, then blew her nose hard.

'It's not fair, it really isn't. All I did was tell them what had to be said and they blew their tops. You'd have thought I'd said we were going to the South of France for a holiday the way they went on.'

George sighed gloomily. It was true; the parents were pretty difficult to get on with, and it wasn't getting any easier.

'They make you say things you don't mean as well. There I was telling them quite calmly that we've got to go go London, then they get all rotten and nowty, and I go and lose my temper.'

George tried not to ask the obvious question but curiosity got the better of him. He whistled when Cynthia told him what she'd said.

'Crikey, what did they do?'

'Three entries, that's what they did. That makes twelve in the last couple of weeks.'

Again George tried to be sympathetic, but again he was too curious.

'What . . . um, what did he give you? Anything . . . ah . . . special?'

The punishment book that Father kept was an awe-inspiring document. It had been started shortly after the accident, and by now it was quite thick. In it were recorded all the bad things the children had done and said, with 'remarks' and a fitting punishment. The punishments were to be put into effect when the parents were their proper size again, and able to supervise. Father was a very imaginative inventor of punishments.

Cynthia's eyes filled with tears again.

'I've got to knit a set of pyjamas for one of the elephants at Belle Vue Zoo,' she said. Cynthia hated knitting. She hated knitting more than practically anything else in the world. Except perhaps elephants. As of now she hated elephants too.

'Wowee,' said George admiringly. 'He is getting nasty. You've already got to do a muffler for one of the giraffes, haven't you?'

'And a bobble-cap for the hippo,' Cynthia said miserably. 'Anyway, that's not all. The other two are worse. I've to wear a skirt for a week – that makes seven in all now – and I'm not to get my first ice-cream of next summer until a month later.'

'When's that make it by?'

'September the twenty-seventh. I'll be lucky if it doesn't freeze to my mouth by then. Oh, Prof, they are difficult to live with. I wish they'd never had the accident!'

It was sad. Before the awful day you couldn't have met two nicer parents. Mother was a dumpy, smiley sort of woman who was always larking about and baking cakes, while Father was great fun, although he spent much too much time thinking about stupid things like nuclear physics. When the children had stood on the moor and seen the two of them get smaller and smaller until they almost disappeared it had been a great shock. The Prof hadn't noticed at first. He'd been staring at the 'target' – the big lump of rock that was meant to end up the size of a pebble. That was still there, three hundred yards from the house, as large as ever. The parents, who'd been standing to one side of the shrinking machine, weren't meant, of course, to have got smaller at all.

The Prof put the finishing touches to the Snark and sighed heavily.

'My dear girl, so do I wish it, so do I. But these things happen you know. The march of science is not without its dangers. Progress, my child, progress.'

Now any talk of progress, and science, was apt to make Cynthia see red. She was a bit of a bad-tempered girl at the best of times, and she *had* just been put three times in the punishment book.

'Progress!' she shouted. 'Progress! How can you sit there and talk about progress when my Mum and Dad are living in a doll's house! Why don't you *do* something about it? *That* would be progress.'

George said quietly: 'Oh stop it, Cynth, stop it. Not another row today. There's just too many of them. Why is it, Prof? Why do we always seem to be rowing these days?'

The Prof put the Snark gently to the floor and switched him on by scratching behind his ear. The dog twitched and looked round before slinking miserably into a corner. He hated being switched off. It would take him some time to recover.

'Well, George, you know it's the strain of it all, I think,' he said. 'We've lived with this problem for too long now and the strain is beginning to tell. The parents are getting more and more cross and so are we.'

'But why does Dad make it worse all the time with that one-man twenty-six piece band and his rotten Hail Smiling Morn? It's driving Mum round the twist. You can't talk to her now without her snapping at you.'

'Think of it this way, George,' the Prof answered. 'If you were reduced to that size, would you want to do something to prove you were as big as anyone else? You would, wouldn't you? That's why your father concentrates on volume, not a wider variety of tunes. We must forgive him, although it's putting us all on edge.'

Cynthia sniffed.

'Perhaps he's doing it on purpose,' she said. 'Perhaps he thinks it's the only way to make you invent a cure, by driving you potty with his row.'

The Prof smiled.

'Perhaps,' he said. 'And find a cure we certainly must, before he does exactly that. Because the strain doesn't make *you* any easier to get on with, my dear, and that upsets me as much as anything.'

George thought there might be some more tears before long, so he got practical, fast.

'Right you are, then,' he said briskly. 'Let's get a move on then, shall we? Let's get down to London and see the Government.'

Soon the whole kitchen was in a fine state of bustle, with the last end of loaf being made into a sandwich, flasks of tea being filled, provisions for the parents and Viva the unreliable cat being sorted out. The Snark was to go with them, and ran around barking with excitement, getting in everyone's way. The planning of an expedition was more than enough to get him over his bad mood.

They'd been at it for a couple of hours when a thought came to George. He stopped the Prof and sat him down on a kitchen chair.

'Just one thing we seem to have forgotten,' he said. 'If you're stony broke, how are we going to get down to London?'

Oh dear. The Prof, unfortunately, hadn't thought of that. He scratched his bald spot for quite a few minutes, then looked in his wallet. There wasn't even a postage stamp. After a few more minutes he pointed towards an ancient railway carriage standing in a corner of the back yard.

'I suppose we'll have to try the cheap day return transferer,' he said.

Cynthia had come into the room halfway through this sentence. Her smile faded like snow in the sunshine. She stamped her foot, going an odd beetrooty colour.

'No!' she said. 'No, no a thousand times no! Prof will you *never* learn?'

He hung his head.

'But what is the alternative, my dear? We have no money. And in any case, the average engineer could *build* a train cheaper than the return fare to London.'

Cynthia grabbed his beard and shook it rudely.

'You have the cheek to sit there and suggest we go off in one of your potty machines when the parents are sitting in the back room the size of gerbils! Isn't one disaster enough! Don't you scientists *ever* learn?'

The Prof unscrambled his beard from her fingers with dignity.

'My dear girl, that machine is not potty. It could well prove to be a boon to mankind. A return trip from anywhere to anywhere in the twinkling of an eye at a cost of pennies. Potty indeed!'

'But it's not been *proved*!' shrieked Cynthia. 'You claim to have made one successful trip in it and the Snark came back covered in seaweed when he was meant to have been to Macclesfield. I ask you!'

The Prof got positively frosty.

'I won't argue with you, Cynthia. The machine is quite satisfactory in theory. It needs a little more work, I will admit, and in normal circumstances I wouldn't think of using it. But what is the alternative?'

He turned to George.

'George, let the decision be yours. You are neither so excitable nor so impolite as your sister. Do you trust in me and my machine?'

George, put on the spot, went slowly red. He looked at the floor. He muttered. At last he spoke.

'Well you must admit, Prof,' he began.

The Prof interrupted, obviously *very* hurt, but trying not to show it.

'Very well, then. I am overruled. But how, may I ask, do you suggest we get there?'

George coughed and looked shy.

'Well,' he said quietly. 'I suppose we'll have to hitch.'

A Normal Night

The sight of a bent old man in a raglan overcoat and spats, covered in mud and standing beside a lonely moorland road in the rain, is a pretty unusual one for a motorist. When he's with two children wearing clothes that look even odder, plus an electronic dog, it would be enough to put anyone off. Every time the three thumbs went up – which wasn't often, because you don't get much traffic on the small winding roads over the moors these days – the approaching car seemed to go faster.

They'd almost given up hope, in fact, and were working themselves up for the long wet trek back across the swampy grassland to think again, when a lorry loomed up out of the rain. Out went the thumbs, past went the truck. Then it slowed down and stopped. The Snark barked. Cynthia yelled, and they all loped up to the cab.

Inside it was hot and dry. The Prof took off his overcoat, the Snark curled up on the engine casing and went to sleep, and the children began to steam gently. The driver looked curiously at them, and obviously would have liked to have asked questions. But the noise inside a lorry cab is amazing, and it's much too tiring to hold a shouted conversation for long.

The children did look pretty odd, though, there was no doubt about that. Instead of normal clothes, like jeans and an anorak say, they had on their Yorkshire Moors Winter Thermals. These were suits of a special material invented by the Prof that kept you warm and dry in all sorts of weather. Your feet didn't stick out of the bottoms of the

legs, like in trousers, but stayed inside. And the hands, too, were in one piece, like gloves, although these could be unzipped if you wanted to count money, or play the piano or something. On top there was a hood that could be pulled right around the face. They were lovely to wear. But looked pretty odd.

It wasn't strictly winter yet, but it certainly felt like it, so they didn't mind their Thermals. In fact, if they hadn't had them they'd probably have frozen to death waiting for a lift.

Luckily, the lorry driver was going all the way to London. They drove through the mists and rain of the high moors, past Holmfirth and through New Mill, and joined the M1 at Junction 37, near Barnsley. Then it was a straight road, all the way down. What's more, once they'd got down to lower ground, the weather cleared up considerably. George and Cynthia were pretty thirsty and roasted when the lorry driver stopped at a service area for a cup of tea.

He guessed from the way Cynthia said she didn't want one that they had no money, so he insisted that they all have a cup on him. As they'd forgotten their thermos

flasks, of course, they accepted gratefully. While they were drinking they tried to explain about their funny clothes.

But the man just fell about.

At last they reached the end of the M1, in North London. They'd decided to go to Mill Hill to stay with friends for the night so there was not much problem, as Mill Hill's just down the road. In fact the lorry driver went slightly out of his way to drop them at the roundabout called Mill Hill Circus. He laughed even harder when Cynthia asked if there were any elephants there. It was a nice goodbye.

The children were quite frightened by it all, one way and another. The traffic was amazing, even more amazing than the motorway. The buildings, too; they'd never seen so many buildings – and the Prof said this was only the outer suburbs. The heat was a problem. It seemed to be lots hotter than the Yorkshire Moors. One thing the Thermals weren't good for was hot climates. They stood on the roadside sweating.

'I thought you said we were going to stay at a farmhouse, Prof,' said George. 'Is that your idea of a joke? This is the middle of the city!'

'Ah,' said the Prof. 'That's the trouble with London. It spreads. Not so long ago Mill Hill was all farmland. And we *are* going to stay in a farmhouse. It's behind that row of shops. The only trouble is, it's not got a farm to go with it anymore.'

Sure enough, just down from the circus, surrounded by modern semis, there was the most beautiful old farmhouse, build of brick, with lots of small-paned windows. There were lights on in all of them, too, although it was hardly dark yet.

'Why are all the lights on?' whispered Cynthia, as they waited while the Prof rang the bell. 'How many people live here? It must be millions.'

The Prof laughed.

'Just my two friends,' he replied. 'And two little boys and

a dog. You're in London now, not Yorkshire. They do things differently down here.'

They certainly did. The door was opened by a short chubby man with a beard, who was holding a glass. A blast of heat poured out into the autumn air, and a blast of noise attacked their ears. The television was on, there was a radio or record-player blaring out music, a dog was barking, and there were yells and shouts coming from somewhere upstairs.

'Hello, Prof,' the short man shouted. 'Have a drink. Glad you could make it! Hello, you kids. Jugears and Mophead are upstairs.'

George and Cynthia looked at each other. 'Glad you could make it'? The Prof had only decided to stay there because it was so late. No one had known they were coming.

The short man shouted again. 'Three more for grub, Mabel. The Prof's arrived with the two moorland brats.'

He ushered the Prof off towards a room, leaving the children confused and lonely in the hall.

But not for long. Suddenly down the stairs shot a small bundle of ginger fur, barking like mad. The Snark sized it up for a second or two, then the dogs leapt on each other, fighting joyfully.

Then a thunder of football boots and two small boys arrived at the foot of the stairs. One had blonde straight hair, the other blonde curly hair. One was in the strip of Leeds United, the other in Tottenham Hotspur. They were both bright red and panting. Cynthia and George held hands.

'Hi,' said the oldest. 'I'm Jugears. That little squirt's my brother. He's called Mophead because of his pretty little curls. He's soppy.'

'Yah you're soppy yourself,' said Mophead defiantly. 'He's called Jugears because of his ears,' he added. 'They're just like jug handles under that hair.'

'Who are you, anyway?' said Jugears. 'Why are you wearing baby-clothes? Can you fight?'

George said quietly: 'They're not baby-clothes. They're special inventions to keep you warm. They're called—'

Mophead interrupted him.

'They're soft,' he said to Jugears. 'Special inventions! I reckon—'

Cynthia hit him hard and Mophead fell to the ground with a shout of surprise. Jugears leaped on Cynthia and George leaped on both of them. The dogs forgot their private quarrel and followed Mophead into the battle. It was fantastic. By the time Mabel and Cedric (the grown-ups) forced them to the tea-table they were all the greatest of friends.

All in all it was a fabulous night, although the Prof didn't enjoy it as much as the children. For a start it was about a thousand times noisier than the house on the moors – Hail Smiling Morn or no Hail Smiling Morn. Then he absent-mindedly tried to switch off Dougal because he was barking so much and got bitten for his pains. Then Cedric and Mabel kept filling his glass up from a green bottle and little bottles and the ice-tray, and he said he was quite sure he'd end up with a headache. It was too hot for him, too, and he didn't like the television, and he wasn't exactly sure he liked George and Cynthia being so friendly with Jugears and Mophead, who thought of nothing but fighting and football. No, the Prof's evening wasn't a real success.

When they were in bed, all piled in the bunks in the boys' room, Cynthia whispered to George: 'Hey, George, isn't it great here?!'

'Fantastic,' said George. 'Oh, Cynth, wouldn't it be lovely to be normal . . .'

CHAPTER FIVE

Two Telephone Calls

The next morning was even more normal, in a way that was even more weird and exciting for George and Cynthia. Instead of cold noses, and steamy breath, and wondering where the night's haul of dead mice might have been left by Viva the unreliable cat, they woke in a warm – a very warm – noisy house, and they woke to the smell of breakfast.

The luxury of not having to draw water from the well (the Prof, unfortunately, never invented practical, simple things, like a way of fixing taps in the house), the luxury of not having to wrestle with the inefficient breakfast machine, the luxury of actually sitting down at a table and being served with food someone else had cooked, was all too much for Cynthia.

'Oh, Prof,' she said. 'Isn't it lovely! Why can't we live like this!'

The Prof, who was hunched up in a silky dressing gown that was too short for him and showed his bony old knees, made a very grumpy noise indeed. He seemed to growl, staring at the kitchen table.

Cedric let out a hoot of laughter.

'I wouldn't talk to him if I were you, dear,' he said. 'I think the Prof's feeling a little bit fragile this morning.'

They started off with fruit juice, then there was cereal, then there was bacon and eggs with lots of toast. Butter and marmalade lay about in dishes. Cynthia and George could hardly believe their eyes, although Jugears and Mophead didn't appear to think there was anything special about it. In fact Mophead caused a row because his favourite cereal had run out. But to the 'moorland brats' it was like a great, wonderful feast.

As they ate, the Prof gradually got back to normal. Cedric and Mabel asked him what they'd be doing all day.

'Well first of all,' he replied, 'I'll have to make a phone call to the Government, if that's all right by you?'

'Go ahead,' said Mabel. 'Anything you like. Treat the house as your own.'

'Thanks. Then I hope we'll be invited along to see them. That's the next step.'

'What do you want to see the Government for?' asked Jugears.

'Don't speak with your mouth full, dear,' said Mabel.

'Excuse my pig, he's a friend,' said Mophead.

'Keep your nose out of other people's business,' said Cedric.

Cynthia started to give a polite answer to Jugears' question, but the Prof shook his head at her. She went bright red.

'Well go on then,' said Jugears. 'What for? Is it a secret?'

The Prof coughed. Mabel and Cedric told the boys not to pry. George and Cynthia felt terrible. They didn't know it was secret. They didn't want secrets from their friends, anyway. They liked them.

'Yes, boys,' said the Prof. 'For the moment it'll have to be a secret I'm afraid. You don't mind too much, do you?'

Mophead pouted.

'It's not fair,' he said. 'Why don't we ever have smashing secrets? Why don't we go to see the Government? *We've* got to go to boring old school. Why don't George and Cynth go to school?'

'Yeah,' said Jugears. 'It's not fair. Nothing ever happens to us. They get all the fun.'

Most strange! Cynthia and George looked at each other. They'd give their left arms to swap places with the boys. Even school would be a nice change.

Anyway, school it was, and work for the grown-ups, and the bustle and hustle of everyone getting ready. There was noise and a lot of coming and going for a while, then the house suddenly empty and amazingly quiet. Quiet, that is, until an odd noise slowly made itself heard. A vague, monotonous hum that wasn't really loud, but somehow filled the air.

'What's that, Prof?' Cynthia said.

'The traffic. Thousands of cars. Buses, lorries, trains. It's London going to work. Strange, isn't it?'

'Well,' said George. 'It's not like the Yorkshire Moors, and that's a fact!'

One of the oddest – and the nicest – things about the London farmhouse was the telephones. Instead of there just being one in the hall or wherever, there were three. So when the Prof phoned the Government, the children each went to a bedroom, and listened to the conversation.

Getting through wasn't all that easy. In fact it took ages and ages. Every time they got on to someone and the Prof explained his business, the person began to sound shifty

and to claim it was nothing to do with him. After a couple
of minutes he'd brighten up a lot and give them someone
else's name. This person, he'd say, was definitely the one to
deal with the Prof. Then he'd say 'I'll put you through'.
There'd be a few clicks and a long silence. Another voice
would come on the line. The Prof would explain his
business. And sure enough, the voice at the other end
would sound shifty, and within minutes the call would be
switched to someone else.

Cynthia's mind had wandered off on to how on earth
Jugears and Mophead could ever get fed up with such a
fabulous life, when at last one of the voices admitted that it
knew the Prof and that it might be able to deal with him.
The Prof explained the problem and asked if he could
come and see someone about it.

It was a simple enough thing to ask, you would have
thought, but the humming and hahing that went on was
amazing. The voice at the end of the telephone kept
bringing up the business of the Monkey Machine.* The
Prof kept insisting that that was all over now, and that
anyway it hadn't been his mistake, but he couldn't make
the voice drop it. The Prof was quite obviously trying his

*See The Great Government Monkey Business Mystery. (Unfortunately
not yet written – J.N.)

hardest to keep his temper, but it wasn't easy. Something to do with last night's green bottle, the children
guessed.

Finally the voice agreed that the Government perhaps
had really better see the Prof, whoever's fault the Monkey
Machine business had been. But it was still a very
frosty, unfriendly voice, and when the Prof mentioned the
children, it blew its top. They all listened in amazement
as it ranted and raved away. They would see the Prof,
yes! Under protest! But *not* the children! Children had
nothing to do with Governments, nothing! Children had
nothing to do with grown-ups! Children had nothing to do
with *anything*! Children should be seen and not heard!
Children should be *not* seen and not heard! Children
should not *be*!

When it had finished ranting it put the phone down with
a bang. Back in the kitchen, the three of them looked at
each other in dismay.

'Well they're *our* parents,' said Cynthia bitterly, 'and
you're not going to see the Government without us. And
that's flat.'

'Absolutely,' George agreed. 'How dare they talk about
us like that? And what's all this about the Monkey
Machine? That's history. We're going and that's final.'

The Prof didn't try to argue.

'I must admit, children,' he said, 'I'd rather take on the
whole Government than leave you here. Those dreadful
boys might come back early. And I will *not* have you spend
another day with them. We'll phone the Thinks Computer.'

When they got through, the computer kept asking them
to speak up. It wasn't hard to tell why. The strains of Hail
Smiling Morn were louder than ever before. Cynthia and
George knew they'd have to do something soon or the
neighbours would start to complain. And they lived eight
miles away!

They waited anxiously, listening to the brass band,

while the computer thought. At last it clicked, coughed, cleared its throat as usual, and shouted this advice:

> I sometimes wonder if you know
> I sometimes wonder if you think
> I sometimes wonder what you'd do
> If you were once without me.
>
> This problem, like so many that
> This problem, like so many what
> This problem, like so oft before
> Is nothing but a bore.
>
> You ask me this, you ask me that
> You ask me not about that cat
> You ask me not why one fat rat
> And fourteen mice upset me.
>
> And all around the kitchen floor
> And all around behind the door
> And all around elsewhere for all
> I know she's gone and laid them.

'What's it *talking* about?' said Cynthia.

'Sshh, sshh,' said George and the Prof.

The computer coughed at the interruption, then started again, in a different rhythm.

> Oh well, as they used once to say,
> It's advice that earns me my pay.
> For the moment I'll call it a day,
> And let the cat play while the Prof's away.
>
> Your problem, yes, your problem:
> You must try another stance.
> If they won't see two children
> They may fall for romance.

Put one on top the other
Put a wig on top of all
With a beautiful assistant
Their bluff you may well call.

And with a click, the phone went dead.

CHAPTER SIX

The Beautiful
Assistant

'Well,' said the Prof. 'It seems to be our day for being hung up on. What do you think all that was about?'

'Hadn't we better talk in the kitchen,' said George, practical as ever.

They all put down their telephones and met in the kitchen. When they had a cup of coffee in their hands they thought better.

'Viva's obviously being extremely unreliable,' George started. 'I do think you ought to have a look at that cat.'

'Isn't it just typical, though,' said Cynthia. 'You ask it a simple question and it goes on for hours on a completely different subject. I vote if you're going to have a look at anything you have a look at the Thinks Computer.'

The Prof said: 'It is a bit saucy, isn't it? But for the moment I don't think we can afford to be without it. Good advice again, my dears, good advice. And you must admit we'd never have thought of it in a million years.'

They all agreed on that, at any rate. Although their problems weren't over by a long chalk.

'It's all very well saying it's good advice,' said Cynthia, 'but how do we go about it? I mean if I sit on George's shoulders and smile like anything I'm still not going to fool anyone, am I? Beautiful assistant, huh!'

George laughed.

'The legs would be all right,' he said, 'but what about your face? No one's ever accused *you* of being beautiful!'

Cynthia was all for clocking George for that, but the Prof

pointed out that they didn't have any time to mess about.
It was already late morning. And things were very serious.

'Just think of your poor mother for a moment,' he told
them. 'What it must be like for her I cannot imagine. Hail
Smiling Morn almost split my eardrums, and we're more
than two hundred miles away.'

Both children got gloomy. Things did look bad. Cynthia
propped her chin in her hands and George bit his lip.

'Oh come on,' said the Prof in a false jolly voice. 'Never
say die. The idea is a good one. All we've got to do is to
decide how to turn you two rather ordinary-looking
children into a beautiful blonde. Stop moping and start to
think.'

The night before, when they'd arrived, Mabel had been
wearing a long skirt, which Cynthia reckoned was pretty
good although she hated wearing ordinary skirts worse
than anything. She thought about it now.

'What did Mabel have on when she went to work?' she
asked.

George and the Prof hadn't noticed.

'I think it was trousers,' said Cynthia, not sure. 'But
where would she keep her clothes?'

'In the wardrobe,' said George.

The Prof chuckled.

'If I know Mabel, on the bedroom floor,' he said. 'I
remember her mother always used to tell her off about it
when she was a girl. I don't think it made much difference.'

Cynthia tapped her teeth with a spoon. She was
thinking.

'Well look,' she said. 'Would Mabel mind a lot if I went
rooting for some clothes?'

'She said to make ourselves at home,' said George. 'Or
was that Cedric?'

'Anyway,' said Cynthia, 'that was in her house. But her
clothes?'

The Prof looked at his watch and tutted.

'Look, my dears,' he said briskly, 'I suggest we act first

and ask questions afterwards. But I'm pretty sure she won't mind. She doesn't mind most things.'

The dressing up was great fun, but it wasn't really a success. The Snark had to be turned out of the bedroom when he and Dougal started to romp around the children. Then George found he couldn't keep Cynthia on his shoulders and stand steady in women's shoes. For a start, they were lots of sizes too big for him. He also got very hot very quickly in his Yorkshire Moors Winter Thermals.

Cynthia found the skirt, which was actually hung quite neatly over the back of the chair. But even when George propped himself up firmly and held on to the bed-head, she couldn't make the skirt stay up round her. The Prof, who was watching carefully to see if he really could get a beautiful assistant this way, started to get glum. When the children fell to the floor for the third time in a tangle of arms and legs, tempers got lost and a fight seemed about to start.

'It's no good,' said George. 'She's just too fat and stupid. We'll never do it.'

'Fat yourself,' snapped Cynthia. 'If you could stand upright for five seconds instead of falling over I'd be able to tie the skirt up. You're a fool!'

'Children!' shouted the Prof. 'Stop bickering! Try again! We *must* succeed!'

But it was no good. Five minutes later Cynthia and George were panting, red in the face, and hating each other. The bedroom door opened and Mabel walked in. She looked at her crumpled skirt, at the mess all over the place, and laughed.

'What *do* you think you're doing?' she said. 'It's like a bear-garden.'

When the Prof had explained everything and the children had cooled down, Mabel got her coat off and took over. George was inclined to be sulky about the whole thing so she told him to get off his Thermals and put on Mophead's Manchester United strip. That way he wouldn't be too hot, and playing the bottom half of the beautiful assistant would be more fun. She also suggested he wore football boots for balance, with a pair of her tights tied up around his waist in case anyone should glimpse his ankles.

Cynthia didn't think it was fair that George should get to wear football strip. She wanted to go as Oldham Athletic, her local team, but Mabel said the boys didn't have it. And anyway, as she pointed out, very few smart young ladies around London wore football strip to see the Government; not even Oldham Athletic. Cynthia's pouts disappeared when she pulled a bra out of a drawer.

'You *will* have to wear this though, Cynthia,' Mabel said. 'And perhaps you could use a football kit to stuff it with?'

Very soon she had them sorted out. George found standing quite easy in the studded boots, even with

Cynthia on top. Wearing the tights was silly, especially
as he slipped his football socks over them, but he
wasn't at all too hot now the Thermals were off. Cynthia
wore her Thermals, but she had a bra padded with Derby
County, a blue furry mohair jumper which was lovely over
it, and a dress ring from Mabel's little finger on the third
finger of her right hand.

Mabel had stuffed the leg from an old pair of tights and
wrapped it around them to make a pair of false hips, and to
keep them well tied together. When they stood there,
swaying slightly, both she and the Prof said they looked like
the real thing – almost.

'Almost?' came George's muffled voice. 'What's up?
And how am I going to see?'

The problem was Cynthia's head. She had short hair
and looked her age. Which was very young indeed for a
beautiful assistant. Mabel went to a cupboard and brought
back a wig.

'Ah well,' she said. 'It's all in a good cause. Try and take
good care of it though, won't you dear?'

With the wig pulled on over a woolly cap to make her
head bigger, plus a dab or two of lipstick and powder,
Cynthia looked superb. The Prof and Mabel walked round
and round clapping their hands in delight. George got
annoyed.

'What am I going to do?' he shouted. 'It's all very well
you lot saying how smashing Cynthia looks, but what
about me? I can't see. How are we going to get about?'

The top half of the beautiful assistant grabbed a bit of
the bottom half and yanked. It was George's hair. There
was a muffled shriek. The assistant swayed and wobbled.
Her wig nearly came off. It took several minutes to restore
her to calm. Mabel and the Prof told her off, top *and*
bottom.

It was Cedric who solved the question of getting about.
He came in for lunch while they were trying to think of an
answer and it came to him in a flash.

'Why not have Cynthia dig George with her left toe for left, right toe for right, both for stop, both twice for start, three times for sit, four times for stand?' he said.

After a fair amount of practice they got it right. The beautiful assistant swayed as she walked, and if you looked closely you could see funny movements under her skirt where the top half was prodding the bottom. But all in all she looked pretty good. And as Mabel said, it was only the Government that had to be fooled. They lifted Cynthia off, and George was only a little pink, although they'd been at it for some time.

'Lunch now, I think,' said Mabel. 'And then Cedric can run you into the Houses of Parliament. I don't think we'd better risk Miss Peabody on a train and bus trip.'

'Who's Miss Peabody?' asked Cynthia, confused.

'Us you idiot,' said George. 'How do we do?'

CHAPTER SEVEN

The Peculiar Charperson

Unlike most beautiful assistants, who sit in the front with the driver, Miss Peabody lay in the back of Cedric's motor car under an oily cloth. The back seats folded forward so there was plenty of room for her, especially as she was in two pieces. The children moaned about it, but it was no use. Both the Prof and Cedric said it was necessary that she shouldn't be seen until she was joined up and ready to fool the Government.

It was a pity, though, because the drive from Mill Hill to the Houses of Parliament, which took well over half an hour, is an exciting one for people who live on the remote hills of the North. Certainly by the time Cedric pulled to a halt on the embankment of the River Thames, the Prof was looking a trifle green and trembly.

The children heard the engine stop and ended the hair-pulling and pinching game they'd been playing to pass the time.

'Come on, Cynth,' said George. 'Time to become the beautiful assistant.'

It was, of course, not an easy matter, cramped up as they were under the oily cloth. Cedric and the Prof held it up and moved about a lot so as to shield the operation from the stares of people going by, but it was quite a performance getting two children and a lot of grown-up clothes into one piece. When Miss Peabody at last stood beside the car clutching the roof-rack, she was panting like a racehorse and had a bright red face.

Cedric shook his head and looked worried.

'It doesn't look quite so good in the cold light of day,' he said. 'Do you really think you'll fool your way into Parliament like that?'

The Prof reached into the car and brought out a big bottle of lemonade.

'Of course we will,' he said. 'Mabel thought of everything. Here Miss Peabody, have a drink of this.'

The beautiful assistant gulped down lemonade in a very unladylike way, but no one was looking luckily. No one noticed either when she slipped the bottle down to George. A most peculiar sight!

At last they were ready. Cedric wished them luck, reminded them of the code for steering George by, then drove off. He would have liked to have waited for them, but he had to go to work.

The code worked pretty well on the whole, with the bottom half of Miss Peabody only going off in the wrong direction once. That looked odd, but the Prof grabbed her arm and made it look as though his elegant friend had merely tripped on the kerb. The first real test came when they met the big policeman guarding the Government's front door.

'Ello ello ello,' he said, in a policemanly manner. 'What's all this 'ere then?'

The Prof cleared his throat.

'Erhum,' he said. 'I've got an appointment with the Government. They're expecting me. This is Miss Peabody.'

'Charmed I'm sure,' said the policeman. He looked in a little black book.

'Oho!' he said after a minute or two. 'You'll be the Prof, then. Yus. But I don't have no mention of a . . . uhum . . . beautiful assistant, begging your pardon, ma'am.'

Cynthia blushed prettily and gave a nervous giggle.

'No,' the Prof said. 'Well, I didn't think it necessary. After all, you wouldn't expect me to come *without* my assistant, now would you?'

'Ho no!' said the policeman. 'Certainly not. Especially

not an assistant as beaut—well, no, sir, of course not.'

He gave the Prof a card which would let him wander about the Houses of Parliament without being arrested, and opened the door to let them in. He touched his helmet to Miss Peabody. Cynthia, on the spur of the moment, blew him a kiss. The policeman went bright scarlet and closed the door on them in a hurry.

Lots of other people in the corridors of the Houses of Parliament stared at the Prof and his beautiful assistant. One fellow in a trench coat and floppy hat, obviously a secret service man by the bulge under his left armpit, actually whistled. Cynthia, who was getting really big-headed by this time, was so flattered that she gave George the wrong toe signal and banged her nose hard into a statue. The Prof looked pleased.

'Now just keep your mind on the job, Cynthia,' he hissed, 'or you'll spoil everything.'

The three main members of the Government lived in a big big office right in the heart of the building. They were called Mr Grandison Splatt, Mrs Sylvester Savoy, and Doberman Dooley. They were guarded by an absolute bevy of secret service men, plus nineteen very big London policemen. They were sitting at a long shiny table drinking tea. Cynthia thought they all looked very sulky.

'Well,' said the Prof. 'Which one of you wants to hear the problem?'

Mr Grandison Splatt shook his head and chewed moodily on a banana.

Mrs Sylvester Savoy said: 'Oh really? How very interesting.'

Doberman Dooley smiled and nodded.

'Ah,' said the Prof. 'It's your department, is it, Dooley? Good. Well—'

Doberman Dooley interrupted him.

'My department? Good Gosh no! I was merely smiling and nodding. It's a free country, what?'

Mr Grandison Splatt let out a loud 'Huh' then yawned

and scratched himself. Cynthia goggled. She couldn't believe it! Was this the Government?

The Prof tried again, then again, then again. Cynthia could tell he was about to blow his top. He'd never quite got over that green bottle. She put on the best grown-up voice she could muster.

'Excuse me please, your Governmentships, but this matter is *very* urgent. Is there anyone else you could ask to see us? If,' she added cleverly, 'you're too busy yourselves, which anyone can see you are.'

'Hear hear!' said Doberman Dooley.

'Yes we *are* rather busy,' said Mrs Sylvester Savoy.

'Aye,' grunted Mr Grandison Splatt.

After a short huddle they told the nearest secret service man to take the Prof and Miss Peabody to room 396. Then they ordered a fresh pot of tea and some peanuts.

The man in Room 396, it turned out, was the Minister of Extremely Secret Things. He was a small, thin, anxious person, who couldn't sit still. All the time the Prof was telling him about the invention – he didn't mention the accident of course; that would come later – he wandered about the room like a terrier who can smell a rat. He pulled books out of the bookshelves and peered behind them, he turned up the corner of the carpet and peered under it, he even lifted the lid off the teapot and peered into that. Every now and then he turned to the Prof with a nervous smile and muttered: 'Can't be too careful you know. Spies everywhere.'

Miss Peabody had sat herself down in a big armchair, which was useful, because it meant that George got a rest. He sat in the seat, with his feet tucked well in, and Cynthia sat on the back. She was half listening to the Prof, but she was much more interested in the office cleaner.

This person was easily the most amazing charwoman she had ever seen. She was dressed in ordinary charwoman-type clothes, and she was pushing an ordinary upright vacuum cleaner, but Cynthia was certain she was really a man. She had on a print dress with a pinny, a scarf round her head like a turban, rolled-down stockings round her ankles, and down-at-heel carpet slippers on her feet. But her feet were enormous – size twelve at least. And her legs above the stockings were thick and hairy. What's more, her face was big and square, and covered in what looked like stubble. There was no doubt in Cynthia's mind. Mrs Mopp needed a shave!

There was something a little bit odd about the hoover too, although she couldn't put her finger on it. Was it the two revolving spools on the front? She'd never seen anything like them on a vacuum cleaner. More like a . . . ? More like a . . . ? No, she couldn't place it.

Anyway, while the Minister was poking about in a flower vase (he picked up a rose and said 'Testing, testing, one two three four' into it) she beckoned the Prof over.

'I'm worried about the charwoman,' she hissed. 'I think she's a man.'

The Minister pounced.

'What are you whispering about,' he asked angrily. 'Is it a secret? That's my department! I insist that you tell me!'

The Prof went over to him. He whispered in the Minister's ear. The Minister looked shocked. Then angry. Then thoughtful. He shook his head.

'Nonsense, my dear Professor,' he said. 'Quite ridiculous! Carry on with your tale.'

The Prof shook his head.

'It *is* very secret,' he said stubbornly. 'I'll say no more until we are alone.'

The Minister looked as though he might argue, then he shrugged.

'Oh very well, if you're going to be silly,' he muttered. 'All right, Mrs Ponsonby-Smythe,' he said to the cleaning lady. 'You can finish this room later.'

The charlady switched off the vacuum, glowering.

'Vot is up viz you zen, ducks?' she said. 'Hain't I doingk eet right, me old China?'

'You see!' said the Minister triumphantly. 'She's as much a Londoner as I am. Off you go now, dear, there's a good body.'

And he ushered the cleaner through the door.

CHAPTER EIGHT

Three Fatal Mistakes

When he came back to his desk the Minister was bad-tempered.

'Really, Professor, you are a nuisance interfering with my office routine like this. What ridiculous nonsense wanting Mrs Ponsonby-Smythe out of the way. He's a very reliable man.'

'He?' said the Prof. 'I thought you said Mrs!'

'You see!' exclaimed the Minister. 'You just don't understand the workings of the Government. Of course she's a man. Under the meaning of the Act.'

'I'm sorry,' said the Prof, 'but I haven't the faintest idea what you're talking about.'

The Minister tutted.

'Well of course you haven't. But it's very simple. When the Equal Opportunities Act came into force we were no longer allowed to advertise for charwomen or Mrs Mopps or cleaning ladies, call them what you will. We had to advertise for charpersons, and if a man had better qualifications than a woman, we had to employ him.

'On the other hand, of course, there is no such thing as a Houses of Parliament charperson's uniform for a man. And as every person working here has to wear a uniform, the men who became charwomen had to wear the regulation pinny and slippers. Once in the uniform it seemed only right to call them Mrs or ma'am, for politeness. Don't you agree?'

The Prof shook his head slowly from side to side.

'Well,' he said. 'What can I say?'

'Precisely,' said the Minister. 'And that fellow's as good a charlady as I've ever had. Heart of gold, from East London. Lovely piece of Cockney that, eh? She called me "Old China"! Now, let's get back to business.'

The first of the fatal blunders came very soon after they started talking seriously again, and it certainly had something to do with the Prof's bad head and fragile feeling.

Up to the time the peculiar charperson had left he had explained to the Minister all about the machine. He said it could shrink objects or people to a fraction of their normal size, and he pointed out that it had dozens of uses to a government. A whole army, he said, could be put into a medium-sized lorry or aeroplane and transported quickly and easily to anywhere they were needed.

The Minister sat down and peeled a banana.

'All that you've told me has been most interesting, Professor,' he said, 'and I'm sure the Government might like to consider it. But I understood you had a problem. What was it?'

'Ah,' said the Prof. 'The old one, I'm afraid. I need several thousand pounds very urgently, to complete the next stage.'

The Minister scratched himself thoughtfully, nibbling at the fruit.

'The next stage,' he said at last. 'Now what would that be, then?'

The Prof cleared his throat.

'Well,' he muttered. 'These armies I'm talking about. Suppose we've got two hundred thousand men safely transported in a plane and waiting to engage the enemy. Right? Well, they're not going to get very far unless we can make them full size, now are they?'

The Minister nodded his head.

'I see,' he said. 'I see, I see. Professor, you disappoint me. I might have known it. You come here wasting my time with your silly schemes, upsetting my cleaning staff, drinking my tea. And all the while it's a sham. A complete and utter sham.'

The Prof went red. Cynthia gritted her teeth.

'It is *not* a sham,' he said. 'What are you talking about? My machine exists, and it works perf—almost perfectly. I have shrunk—'

'Oh yes, you have *shrunk*!' cried the Minister. 'I'm *sure* you have shrunk, Professor! Nothing simpler! But have you *de*shrunk? *That* is the question!'

The Prof was silent. There was a pause.

'And you,' went on the Minister. 'And you have the cheek to want the Government to bail you out! To put up thousands of pounds. When all you can offer is the way to turn two hundred thousand soldiers into white mice! Oh yes, very nice, I'm *sure*!'

Another pause. Then the Prof spoke.

'A few thousand pounds is all I ask. And then you will have the greatest weapon ever invented. I wish you would think about it.'

'Greatest weapon!' snorted the Minister. 'Like the Monkey Machine, I suppose? *That* was the last greatest weapon you offered us. And what happened? You made monkeys of the lot of us!'

'Oh don't bring that old business up again,' the Prof said angrily. 'That was ages ago. And anyway, I put everyone right again, didn't I?'

'It's the principle that counts,' said the Minister. 'You promised us that we could turn our enemies into friendly fellows who thought of nothing but peanuts and climbing trees, and what happened? You turned half our leading politicians into apes! Some of them are only just getting over it!'

He unpeeled another banana with a furious gesture and the Prof made the first fatal mistake.

'And it was all their fault,' he shouted. 'I begged them not to push ahead so fast. I told them I needed more work doing. I told them I was not ready and needed more money. And what did they do? They *forced* me to give them a demonstration! Anyway, turning a member of the Government into a monkey is all too easy! I suspect some of them were halfway there before I started!'

The Prof stood up abruptly. He was brimming over with rage. He was going to have one of his tantrums. Cynthia closed her eyes and bit her lip. Oh dear oh dear. Blow that green bottle!

The Prof in a tantrum was a terrible sight. He waved his arms, he shook his fists, he stamped his feet, he went bright purple, he swore horribly. When he'd finished dancing about he sat down, panting. The Minister looked at him in a very icy way. He was not pleased.

'Well well, Professor,' he said nastily. 'What a disgusting display of bad manners. Just exactly what I would have expected of you as well. And if you think that sort of thing is going to help you, you've got another think coming!'

Cynthia wrung her hands in agony. The Prof had ruined it all! Oh the poor poor parents!

She made the second fatal mistake.

'Oh Mr Minister,' she said, her voice shaking, 'please, Mr Minister don't mind the Prof. Think of Mum and Dad. What are they going to do if we don't get the money?'

The Minister stood up. He was like a little weasel with pop-eyes. He got icier and icier. His voice was almost frozen.

'Mum and Dad?' he asked. 'Mum and Dad?! What sort of a statement is *that* from a beautiful assistant?'

It may have been the lack of Winter Thermals or it may have been the iciness of the Minister; whatever the cause was George, at this moment, made the third and final blunder. He sneezed.

It wasn't just an ordinary sneeze, although that would have been bad enough. It was a monster sneeze, a giant sneeze, an enormous sneeze. Cynthia jumped a foot in the air and fell over the back of the chair. There was a ripping noise and a shriek as she took half the long skirt with her.

And there was George. Wearing a silly grin, a Manchester United No. 7 strip, a pair of tights with holes in them – and football socks and boots.

Two minutes later they were all in Parliament Square. The Minister had thrown them out.

CHAPTER NINE

Lucky Break

Back home in Yorkshire things went from black to blacker to blackest. Even the weather seemed determined to make their lives miserable. When a friendly motorist dropped them back on the moors an early cold snap had covered everything in a thin sheet of frozen snow. As they trudged from the road to the house their boots crackled in the frost. First Cynthia, then the Prof, then George, went through ice patches into pools of freezing water. With soggy feet even the Winter Thermals couldn't keep them warm for long.

The house was dreadful. After the warm, dry, noisy farmless farmhouse in Mill Hill it seemed a thousand times worse than it normally did after being left for a spell. The trouble was its age, and the moorland weather. It was nearly three hundred years old, and as George remarked, it looked as though it had been empty for about two hundred and fifty of them, although they'd only been away a couple of days. It was damp, with ice patches on the insides of the walls, and the draughts that howled through every room were only slightly less chilly than the wind roaring across from the north-east coast. They rushed about like mad things getting fires lit, but they made no impression for hours. The only way you could tell the place was warming up was because the furniture began to steam.

'Dream cottages on the moors,' said Cynthia miserably as she broke the ice in the kettle with a fork. 'You can keep them!'

Viva the unreliable cat had added her share to the

chaos. She'd carefully hidden her catch of mice (plus one rat) in the most unlikely places. Two in the oven, one on the kitchen mantelpiece, three in Cynthia's best woolly hat, one in the teapot. The Prof gave her blacker and blacker looks. When he found one in his tobacco jar he reached for his screwdriver. But Viva, who was quick if nothing else, disappeared like a shot from a gun.

Worst of all, of course, was telling the parents. Cynthia utterly and completely refused to do the job on her own, and George pointed out to the Prof - rather unfairly - that

as it was all his fault he ought to do the dirty work himself. The Prof got very huffy and started to sulk, until Cynthia took George to one side and nagged at him till he apologised. At last they agreed to go all together.

Mabel had given them a supply of food to tide them over, so they took a thermos of soup and some posh biscuits along. But as they walked through the cold dank corridors they didn't have much hope that these offerings would make the parents take the news any better.

Strangely enough, Mother and Father accepted the tale of the disaster fairly mildly - at first. They were, after all, not affected by the weather like the others. They were warm and snug in their centrally-heated doll's house, with no worries about draughts, damp, ice or mice. They seemed to take pity on the Prof and the two children who stood in front of them shivering and sniffling, practically with icicles on their noses.

But by the next day, all that had changed. When it sank in that the expedition had not only failed to get the money that was needed but had succeeded in making sure the Government would never listen to them again, the parents' tempers went downhill very fast indeed. Cynthia got two entries in the punishment book in quick succession, and George got a particularly nasty one without having done anything at all.

What was worse, Father went into a decline and manufactured another tune for the one-man twenty-six piece brass band. This one was the Posthorn Gallop, and he played it morning, noon and night, louder and louder. What's more, he made a mistake in the last solo part, always in the same place, always at the same time. The tune, shrilly ringing out time after time, hour after hour, with the mistake always dead on cue, frayed everyone's nerves to snapping point. As for Mother, it was awful. She became very morose, and never opened her mouth except to tell them off. And she went through ice almost as fast as the fridge could make it.

Even the Thinks Computer appeared to have gone slightly dippy. Maybe it was the cold. They all trooped in one morning and said nice things about it and pretended to be jolly and great friends and remarked how good it was looking. But when the Prof typed out a question and fed it in the answer was just silly. It whirred and flashed, cleared its throat, and said:

> You don't give a rap for anyone
> You ask daft questions and think it's fun
> An elephant at least would get a bun
> After doing for you what I have done.

They looked at each other in amazement.

'What's it talking about?' hissed Cynthia. 'What's it done that's so wonderful?'

'I'm hanged if I know,' muttered the Prof. 'What's all this nonsense about buns?'

It was practical George who guessed the answer. He snapped his fingers.

'I know! We haven't even told it its first plan didn't work! It probably just thinks we're being greedy – and ungrateful!'

Cynthia was all for the Prof typing out a piece of his mind about the last hare-brained scheme, but the other two hushed her up quickly. Not quickly enough perhaps though, because when the Prof typed out an explanation and asked what they ought to do now, having failed once, the Thinks Computer was positively rude.

> That's right, blame me you silly lot.
> Oh yes I know that *I'm* the clot!
> It's all my fault when you upset
> My plans for raising money!
>
> Well listen now, it's your last chance
> I won't be led another dance.
> If you don't get it right this time
> I'll leave you in the mire.
>
> Walk seven paces to the north
> And twenty paces to the west
> And fourteen paces to the south
> And then get down to digging.
>
> If you don't find an oil well
> Your clothes and boots you'll have to sell
> Or else that cat, she'd fetch a lot
> And I for one won't miss her.
>
> Or else you could rob a bank
> Or else you could win the pools

Or else you could marry a millionaire
But leave me alone you fools!

There was a short pause, then the 'End of Message' light came on.

'Well really!' Cynthia exploded.

The Thinks Computer made a noise that was extremely like a laugh. Not a friendly one, either. The Prof and George hustled Cynthia into the kitchen before she tried to do the machine a mischief.

By the fifth morning the situation was ruinous. Cynthia refused to get up, although it was her turn to make breakfast, the noise of the Posthorn Gallop, complete with mistake, was rattling the stone slates on the roof, and the Prof was refusing to talk. He spent every available hour in his inventing room, struggling to solve a problem. Not *the* problem, though, oh no! The Prof, too, was being sulky and unhelpful and downright silly. He was trying to invent a way to cheat at chess. George was in despair.

As he sat in the kitchen, watching his tears plop off the end of his nose into the mug of tea, the door was scratched open and the Snark bounded in. It was beginning to thaw now, and he was soaking wet. But the newspaper was bone

dry, and there was a letter sticking from the electronic mouth too. He rushed up to George, tail wagging, and dropped them on the floor. George absent-mindedly patted his head. He put down his tea and picked up the letter. It was only a circular, sent round to everyone he guessed, but they didn't often have anything at all. He tore it open, his tears forgotten.

It was a single sheet of paper, badly typed on one side only. It was smudged, hard to read. George went over to the window to get the extra light.

'GOT A PROBLEM?' it said in capitals at the top. 'Need money?' 'Want help to sort something out?' George blinked. Hey, this just might be the answer!

The circular was so smudgy that he couldn't read all of it. But it appeared that there was a firm that lent people lots of money without asking too many questions. This firm also helped people in trouble. It made the point, too, that it was especially used to sorting out problems that were deadly secret. 'We promise not to tell,' the circular ended up.

George was really excited now. Where were the offices?

At the bottom, in big letters, it said: 'IF YOU WANT HELP, APPLY TO MISTER FIXIT. WE TRAVEL THE WORLD IN OUR CARAVAN. THIS WEEK WE ARE ON THE YORKSHIRE MOORS.'

And it gave the name of a place George knew.

It was a crossroads only two miles from the house.

What an incredible stroke of luck!

CHAPTER TEN

George Goes it Alone (Almost)

George looked out of the window at the rapidly melting snow, but he hardly saw it. His mind was miles away. He was with Mister Fixit. He was being given bundles and bundles of five-pound notes. He was rich. And soon the parents would be all right again.

He shook himself out of the dream, grabbed the delighted Snark up from the floor and hugged him, finished his tea in one gulp. Then he hared up the stairs as fast as his legs would take him.

'Cynthia!' he shouted. 'Cynth! Get up! Wake up! Some fantastic news!'

The lump under the blankets squirmed, but her head didn't appear. George stuck his finger in, hard. There was a muffled squeak.

'Come on, Cynth! Quick! We can do it! We can save the parents!'

Slowly Cynthia pulled down the covers. Slowly her face came out from under the pile. She was pouting, and red-faced, and bad-tempered.

'What's all the row about anyway? I'm *not* getting up and that's final. I'm fed up with the whole thing. Fed up!'

'Oh shut up moaning and listen,' cried George, waving the circular. 'Look at this. Look at it, will you!'

She took the paper and sat up, shivering slightly. George jumped from one foot to the other while she went through it. At last Cynthia dropped it onto the bed and slumped down again.

'Well?' he said.

'Well what?' she replied. 'What did you wake me up to show me that rubbish for?'

'Rubbish!' George shrieked. 'Can't you read, you twit! It says money lent with no questions. Problems solved in secret! What are you on about?'

Cynthia tried to pull the covers back over her head but he stopped her.

'Don't be soppy, George,' she said. 'No one's going to lend *us* money. That means *people*. *Grown*-ups. They don't go around giving money to the likes of us.

'Anyway,' she added. 'How would we pay them back?'

George was almost speechless. What a great sulky lump! Couldn't recognise a stroke of luck if it hit her in the eye!

'Well!' he said. 'You rotten little moaning Minnie! I'll jolly well do it without you and you can say what you like! Just go back to sleep!'

She pulled the covers over her head. George shrugged, picked up the paper, and left.

He began to get worried, though, when he couldn't make the Prof see sense either. He went into the inventing room almost as bouncily as he'd gone to see Cynthia. The Prof didn't even grunt.

'Prof,' said George. 'A letter came this morning. The Snark brought it back from the Post Office. With the paper.'

The Prof was sitting at his workbench, glaring at a peculiar chess set. The pieces were luminous, and kept moving about the board without being touched. The Prof kept going 'Hhmm' and 'Hah'. He didn't look up.

'It was very interesting,' said George. 'I've got it here. Would you like to read it?'

The Prof flapped his hand irritably.

'Go away, go away!'

George bit his lip.

'I'll read it out to you,' he said. 'Listen: "Got a problem? Need money? Want help to—"'

The Prof banged his workbench with his fist.

'George,' he shouted, '*will* you leave me in peace! How many more times do I have to tell you not to disturb me in my inventing room?'

'But Prof! This letter! Mister Fixit! I think it's the answer! They'll give us money!'

A luminous knight moved jerkily across the board and started flashing like a small beacon.

'Ah!' said the Prof, beaming. 'Check mate, I think! And it wasn't even his move!'

George ran from the room, defeated.

He sat moodily in the kitchen for a long while, listening to the sounds of the old house and wondering what to do. It was no use consulting the Thinks Computer at the moment, because he knew it would only give a stupid or cheeky answer. The Snark, it seemed to him, was the only one with half a brain in the house, and the Snark couldn't talk. He chewed his nails. What a hopeless lot! What a terribly hopeless lot!

It slowly dawned on him that he could actually *hear* the house. It creaked and groaned a little in the wind. Nothing odd about that – it always did. So what was different? It came in a flash. No Posthorn Gallop. No Hail Smiling Morn. Father must be asleep.

Before he fully knew he was doing it, George had opened the door to the first passage and was hurrying towards the back room where the parents lived. He'd risk the punishments book. He'd risk Mother nagging. If Dad was asleep there was just a chance he could get some sense out of her.

He opened the last door quietly and tiptoed over to the doll's house. With an eye to the bedroom window he could see his father flat out on the bed with a tiny handkerchief over his face. Lazy pig thought George, but he was mighty glad. Normally he'd have been making a row for his breakfast long ago. He looked into each window in turn till he spotted Mum. She was in the lounge reading.

George tapped with his fingernail. Mother came to the window, pulled up the sash and poked her head out.

'What time do you call this to bring breakfast, you bad boy?' she snapped.

'Ssh! Don't wake up Dad,' George hissed. 'Listen, Ma, I think I can save you. I've found a place to get money!'

Mother's eyes lit up. She stopped nagging immediately. As George explained everything she got more and more excited.

'Well, George,' she said finally. 'I never knew you were such a smart boy. It sounds perfect. And I'll tell you what – I'm coming too!'

George goggled.

'Coming too? What, coming with me to see Mister Fixit? Do you think you should, Mum?'

'Why not indeed?' she answered. 'If everyone else is too sulky or too silly I don't see why I shouldn't. In any case, I'd give anything to get away for an hour or two, anything. If I hear the Posthorn Gallop once more I think I might explode. Hang on, I'll get on my coat and hat.'

Two minutes later she appeared at the front door, well wrapped up. George picked her up carefully and headed back towards the kitchen, where she sat on the table nibbling bread while he made her a woolly nest in a shopping bag. When everything was ready he scribbled a note for the Prof and Cynthia.

But as he was going through the back door, George changed his mind. They didn't deserve a note, he thought. They were a pair of spoilt babies and it would do them good to stew in their own juice. Then when he came back in triumph, carrying thousands of fivers, they'd really feel sorry. They'd really wish they hadn't been such idiots.

He laughed aloud as he tore the note up into tiny pieces. The Snark gave a low whine, as though warning him. But

George just laughed more. He chucked the pieces of paper into the fireplace, picked up the shopping bag again, snuffed the cold air at the back door, then set out over the moor to find the caravan.

CHAPTER ELEVEN

Kidnapped

Although the thaw was well under way it was still mighty cold on the moors. For the first half mile or so mother chattered brightly. It was the first time she'd been out of the doll's house for a long while, let alone out of doors. Everything was new and exciting to her – the snow-capped peaks, the frozen pools, the grey clouds speeding across the sky like racehorses. George talked back as much as he could, but despite his Thermals and the hard work he was doing trudging through the boggy, steep countryside, he was soon shivering.

Even Mother, well wrapped up and snuggled into the nest of wool, began to feel the bite of the air after a while. At last she stopped talking, stopped pointing out odd-shaped rocks and soaring birds, and burrowed into the warmth. George trudged on.

The trouble with moors is that even in summer they tend to be boggy. Now, close to winter, they were almost flooded in places. George had to keep walking in huge circles to get to the point straight in front of him. After more than an hour he was still a long way from where the caravan was meant to be parked. And he was very tired.

But when he was climbing the last slope, all his tiredness slipped away. He was almost there! Soon he'd have the money. He wiggled his finger in the nest.

'Hey, Mum! One more hill! Come out and watch!'

His mother poked her tiny head out and peeped over the shopping bag. George clambered rapidly to the top of the rise and they stared at the road below.

There in a lay-by just off from the crossroads, was a big white caravan. It had a crooked chimney sticking through the top, with smoke pouring out and streaming away in the wind. In front of the van was a Land Rover.

'Hooray!' shouted George. 'We've made it. You just pop back inside, Mum, and keep well hidden. We don't want anyone to see you just yet, now do we?'

The curtains of the caravan were all drawn, and there was not a sound to be heard as he walked along the lay-by towards it. If it hadn't been for the smoke he would have thought it was empty. No notice saying 'Mister Fixit', no queues of people collecting bundles of fivers. Nothing. George began to feel nervous.

He went round to the side away from the road and found the doorway. He tapped gently. Nothing. He knocked louder. Still nothing. He knocked very loudly indeed, then got ready to go away. They must be out.

Suddenly the door shot open, making him jump. A big man, a huge man, with very short hair and a stubbly chin appeared. He yawned enormously. Must have been asleep. He stared down at George.

'Vot ees eet you vant, leedle poy?' he said.

George's voice was trembling.

'Please, sir,' he said. 'I want to talk to Mister . . . to Mister Fixit.'

The huge hairy man threw his head back. He gave a sort of hooting laugh. George nearly died.

'Hah!' he roared. 'Zat didn't take ferry long, did eet? Come in, leedle poy! Mister Feexeet he be pleased to seeing you!'

George had a strange feeling right down in his stomach that he'd made a bad mistake. He suddenly knew that he'd done the wrong thing. He decided to run away.

Too late. As he turned, the giant leaned down and picked him up by the front of his Thermals. Before he could say a word he was inside the van and the door was closed.

It was very queer. The van was done out like an old pub.

There were wooden armchairs, a dartboard, chintzy sofas. On a scrubbed table some dominoes and a pack of cards lay about. The giant pointed to a chair.

'Seet down, leedle poy. Meester Feexeet he come in a meeneet.'

'Um. Er. Well actually I've changed my mind,' said George. 'I've decided not to see him after all. Goodbye, I'll see myself out.'

He turned round. The big fellow took the top of his head between his finger and thumb and turned him back again.

'Seet down,' he said.

George sat.

A couple of seconds later a door at the end of the room opened. George's eyes popped. The fattest man he had ever seen in his life waddled in. He was completely round, like a ball, with a shiny bald head. He had on a yellow and red check suit that hurt your eyes to look at, with a watchchain spread across his waistcoat that looked about a yard long. He was five feet tall.

He stuck out a hand for George to shake. It was very like a bunch of bananas, only slightly damp.

'Allo, Sonny Jim,' he said. 'I ham Mister Fixit. Pleased to be seeingk you.'

George gulped. He tucked the shopping bag tightly between his ankles, hoping against hope that Mother would keep quiet.

The big man laughed again.

'I am telling heem you will be pleased to see heem, old China,' he said.

George gasped.

'Mrs Ponsonby-Smythe,' he whispered.

But it couldn't be, surely? He looked at the heavy chin and the enormous black boots. Oh dear oh dear. If only he'd been able to see, stuck inside that long skirt.

'Vell, Sonny Jim,' said the fat man. 'How am I to be helping you? You have ze problem, yes?'

'No, no,' George blurted out. 'I was just passing and I thought . . . '

Mr Fixit smiled.

'Don't be frightened, Sonny Jim,' he said kindly. 'My friend is a bit beeg and ugly, but he have got ze heart of gold. Hain't zat true, Charlie?'

A deep chuckle.

'Zat's ze exacting truth,' he said.

George said: 'Is your name really and truly Mister Fixit?'

'Of course it's not. Vot sort of a name is zat eh? I am called Johnnie Smith and my friend here is Charlie Robinson. It is a business name, Fixit. I fixes things for ze peoples.'

George blushed.

'Johnnie Smith and Charlie Robinson are pretty funny names for foreign people,' he said. 'Where do you come from?'

The fat man wobbled his chins with a frown.

'Foreign?' he cried. 'Vere are you getting zat idea from? We are as English as ze next mens!'

'Oh,' said George, confused. 'But your voices? They don't sound very English.'

'Did you not read our advertising? We travel the world to help people. You funny boy, we speak like zis because we are always in the strange lands. Zis week the Yorkshire Moors, next veek – who knows? Have a cup of tea!'

While the giant brewed a pot of tea, Mr Fixit threw darts at the board and explained a bit more. He and his friend, although English to the core, had so many good works to do that they could only be at home for a few days a year. They missed England, but the world needed them badly. He waved a hand round the room. That, he said, was why it was decorated like an English pub; to remind them of home. And they ate nothing but fish and chips and roast beef and scones, and drank tea by the gallon.

As if to prove his point the tea arrived just then, along

with some toasted teacakes and butter. George was even more confused. He'd have loved to have asked Mum what she thought. But the teacakes were nice. And Mr Fixit and Mr Robinson got nicer too, when you got used to their size and shape. He began to think he'd been too hasty.

After a couple of games of Snap and a hand of Happy Families he was sure. And when Mr Fixit steered the talking round to the problem, George told him everything. About the invention, the trip to London, and the need for cash. A huge smile, deep and buttery, spread slowly over Mr Fixit's fat face.

'Well, Georgie,' he said. 'I think ve can help. But of course, ve need some sort of proof zat you're tellingk ze truth. Can you perhaps bring me ze machine, just to haf a look at?'

No no, said George. Out of the question.

'Vell,' said Mr Fixit. 'Could the Prof perhaps bring eet? Somehow ve must see.'

Gosh no, George explained. The Prof didn't even know he was here. The two men looked at each other.

'Vell zen,' said Mr Fixit. 'Ve cannot help you, Georgie. Ve need Prof . . . I mean ve need *proof.* How can I give you thousands of pounds wizout proof?'

'But your circular said . . .'

'*Proof*, Georgie. Ve must haf *proof*!'

George thought hard for a while. The men were still smiling, still very friendly. He was silly not to trust them. Crazy. Anyway, it was now or never: no proof, no money.

'I'll give you proof,' he said. 'Look.'

He reached between his ankles and felt in the woolly nest for his mother.

'George, you *fool*!' she shrieked as he pulled her out of the bag. 'You silly, *silly* fool!'

'Ah,' said Mr Fixit. With a quick movement he grabbed George by the wrist and plucked Mother from his hand. George's mouth fell open in horror.

'Now, little boy,' said Fixit, smiling no longer. 'Get back home double quick. I want zat machine by tomorrow night.'

'But you said . . . but you said.'

'Tomorrow wizout fail. A fair swap I think? Ze machine for your mother. No machine, no mother. Understood?'

The giant picked George up with one hand, opened the door, and held him over the sill.

'Scoot, leedle poy,' he said grimly. 'Ve see you tomorrow. Don't forget, eh?'

And with a crash that shook his bones, George was dropped to the ground as the caravan door slammed shut.

CHAPTER TWELVE

The Plot

For the first time in his life George overtook Cynthia in the punishment book. To say Father was angry is a wild understatement. He blew his top. He flipped his lid. He did his tank. He went hairless. He was so mad that he filled in seven pages of the book without even bothering to tell George what the punishments were. But he was pretty sure he'd not be eating ice-creams or chocolate cake for so long that he'd have grown out of them – or died of old age.

The Prof and Cynthia had no sympathy at all. They were angry too, although George secretly thought it was all their fault for not going with him. Cynthia just couldn't bear to look at him without saying something nasty, while the Prof was even worse in a way. George kept catching sight of him shaking his head and tutting as though he, George, was some terribly low form of life.

But at least the loss of Mother did one good thing: it shook them all up. It got them thinking again. In fact, after the first shock had worn off there was a burst of quite frantic activity.

George started it. They were sitting at the dinner table wincing at the strains of Hail Smiling Morn, so loud now that it shook the knives and forks, and the other two were being quietly rotten to him. Suddenly he banged down his spoon and shouted.

'Well don't just sit there looking like lumps of cold porridge,' he said. '*Do* something!'

The Prof looked surprised. Then he smiled.

'By Jingo, George,' he said, 'you're right. We've *got* to do something.'

'We have,' Cynthia agreed. 'Crikey, a little teeny-weeny mum is better than no mum at all. We've got to get her back.'

George smiled for the first time in hours. At last they were behaving like Cynth and the Prof again.

'What are we going to do?' he asked. 'Give them the shrinker?'

The Prof shook his head.

'Certainly not,' he said. 'Out of the question.'

Cynthia wasn't so sure.

'Well we've got to get her back, Prof. Surely you're not going to be greedy about it. You'd rather have Mum back than a soppy machine wouldn't you?'

'My dears,' said the Prof, 'I certainly would. But don't be childish. If we give them the machine they *might* give us back Mother. They might. But what size would she be? And what size would she remain?'

It was a point. Even with the machine they couldn't get the parents back to normal until they got some money to sort out the deshrinking side of it. But with no machine at all!

'Well what *are* we going to do?' asked George. His smile had gone again. 'We've got to save her. And quick! Apart from anything else, how will she be without her supply of ice?'

'I'm afraid it's beyond the scope of our brains, children,' replied the Prof. 'And your father seems to have decided to hinder rather than help. Which leaves us, I fear, with our friend the Thinks Computer.'

Cynthia snorted.

'Friend! Huh! I'd like to kick it in the slats,' she said.

'Yes, dear, it has been a bit awkward of late. But we must give it a try. Perhaps if we approach it right. Be nice to it. Jolly it along.'

'Flannel it up a bit?' suggested George.

'Precisely,' said the Prof. 'We'll give it so much flannel it won't know what hit it.'

Five minutes later they were all sitting round the computer with big smiles on their faces as the Prof typed a very pleasant request indeed to feed into it. The machine seemed to sense that something was going on. It hummed louder than normal, and the lights on its front flickered brightly and fast. The Prof passed the completed question to George and Cynthia. It mentioned the computer's exceptional cleverness, how good it was to them, what nasty conditions it had to work under in the cold farmhouse, how smart it was at hatching plots, how grateful they'd be if it could get Mother back for them. The children agreed. It was a lovely piece of flannel.

Obviously the Thinks Computer thought so too. After the Prof fed the question into the slot the lights flickered faster and for much longer than usual. The hum went higher and higher and higher and higher. From four feet away George could actually feel the heat from its polished dome. They all waited eagerly, in complete silence, when the 'Ready to Inform' light flashed on. The Prof pressed the 'Clear' button most gently.

The Thinks Computer cleared its throat several times. Its scratchy voice, when it came, sounded disgustingly self-satisfied, even pompous. It sounded, as Cynthia said afterwards, like the cat who's eaten the canary.

This is what it said:

> Aha my friends I see at last
> That bygones are bygones and past is past.
> You've come to recognise my worth
> And that I'm very clever.
>
> About time too is all I'll say
> For I'll not boast or demand that you lay
> Flat on the carpet in homage to me
> But this time don't forget it.

You've really made a terrible mess
To lots of blunders you must confess
But never mind you stupid lot
It is my pleasure to save you.

With my superior brain I reckon
That four to two is a deadly weapon.
That's Prof, two kids and a father short
I'll tell how he can help you.

That row you hear right round the moors
Through three-foot thickness of walls and oak doors.
If military music should chance to be
With terrible dread would fill them.

Now there's your advice and this time see
You don't act daft and disregard me.
The plot is perfect its very plain
So please try to do it proply.

The 'End of Message' light flashed on. The Thinks Computer sighed smugly. Cynthia, George and the Prof stared.

'Well,' said George. 'What a fabulous idea! Good old Thinks Computer!'

'Dad as a military band!' said Cynthia. 'It'll scare them half to death! They'll think the whole Army's after them!'

'A pipe band perhaps,' added the Prof. 'Great hairy Scotsmen in kilts marching across the moors to the strains of Amazing Grace! Oh I say, what a jolly fine idea. Well done, machine!'

The Thinks Computer purred gently. Cynthia burnt her hand patting it on the head as they returned to the kitchen.

Round the table with a pot of tea they worked out the details of the plot. They decided they'd take the Yorkshire Moors Driverless Tractor, and they decided the attack should be at dusk. The tractor, one of the Prof's best inventions, looked something like an ordinary jeep, except that it had legs instead of wheels. On the legs, which were made of bendy steel with joints, there were stout boots and waterproof socks to keep the mechanism warm and dry. It also had an arm sticking out of the right side, which carried a hickory walking stick to help over the roughest bits. On the moors there was nothing to touch it, not even a tank.

'We'll go over there tomorrow afternoon,' said the Prof, 'and hide behind a hill where we can watch the caravan. That way we can make sure the area's deserted, and if one of them should happen to leave for a walk or something, we'll be able to pounce.'

'Then when it gets dark,' said Cynthia. 'We'll attack!'

'We'll black up our faces like commandos,' said George, bouncing up and down. 'Hey, won't it be fantastic!'

'Then with Father well hidden in a safe place and blaring out a rousing march, we'll go in fighting,' cried the Prof.

'They'll be terrified!' shrieked Cynthia. 'They'll die of surprise!'

'We'll grab Mum, nip out to the tractor, hop on board –
and away,' George roared. 'They'll never catch us, never!
Hooray!'

The Prof banged for quiet with his mug.

'Right, children,' he said calmly. 'We have a plan. It will
work. Now let us speak to your father and get everything
ready.'

CHAPTER THIRTEEN

The Mystery

It was very late by the time they'd explained everything to Father and got him to agree. At first he thought the idea was daft, but slowly he got to grips with the problem of turning the one-man twenty-six piece brass band into a military outfit and before long he was as excited as anyone. He decided that Under the Double Eagle, a stirring march, was just the thing, although the Prof reckoned Amazing Grace would make the spies a lot more frightened. Father hummed and hahed, and pointed out that they had no bagpipes. But as it happened, Cynthia did have a very fine toy set, and they finally left Father with both instruments, scratching his head as he tried to make up his mind.

In the morning the activity was feverish. Everyone rushed here and there, sorting out exactly what they needed for the expedition. There were sandwiches to be made, coffee and tea to be brewed and put into flasks, Mother's needs to be thought of. First and most important, she'd have to have some fresh ice. Cynthia got it out of the ice-tray, crushed it up small, and poured it into a thermos.

The question of weapons was raised by George. The Prof was dead against it. Weapons were dangerous, he pointed out, and someone might get hurt.

'But what if they put up a fight?' George demanded. 'We can't just go in empty-handed. One of them's a giant, I told you!'

Cynthia sniffed.

'That'll be Mrs Ponsonby-Smythe, I suppose. Really,

George, you do exaggerate. For a charlady I admit she was a bit on the biggish side, but I expect he's perfectly normal for a spy!'

Faced with an argument like that George could only gasp. The Prof took a firm stand.

'I'm taking a firm stand on this matter,' he said. 'No weapons. If we wade in there carrying guns or something, it'll all go to pot. We have surprise on our side remember. *And* Amazing Grace!'

George pouted.

'Not even sticks? A couple of big heavy sticks in case they turn nasty?'

'Not even sticks. Now don't be difficult, George. We'll do it the way the computer said.'

The computer, as it happened, had been trying to say lots more all morning. Even without being programmed it wanted to stick its oar in. It kept giving out bellows and grunts from the living room, doing its best to attract attention. Whenever anyone went in there for something it would come out with a short rhyme over and over again.

Give me a question, please I pray
I am the greatest and I've something to say.

But they had no time to bother with it, and it obviously just wanted to get in on the excitement.

On the third time Cynthia went into the room, looking for a ball of string, the Thinks Computer whipped out its flexing arm and gave her a hard pinch as she bent over a drawer.

Cynthia let out a cry of pain.

'You stupid thing,' she shouted. 'Shut up will you, we're busy!'

The computer replied:

You're all so thick I think you ought
To listen to me in case you're caught.

Cynthia wasn't too fond of the computer at the best of times. She picked up a sheet and flung it over the thing. There was a sort of squawk, then it shut up – rather like a parrot when you cover its cage.

The Snark, too, sensed the excitement and started making a nuisance of himself. He rushed about barking his head off, he knocked over his drinking bowl, and he kept nipping people's ankles so that they wouldn't forget he was there and leave him behind.

He nipped the Prof's once too often. Out lashed his boot. The Snark yelped, but the Prof yelped louder. There was a blue flash and he got a stiff electric shock.

'Which just goes to show,' said George severely, 'that you shouldn't kick dogs. Not even electronic ones.'

He bent down and patted the Snark.

'There, boy,' he said. 'Never mind the nasty old Prof. But do calm down, we're busy.'

It didn't do much good, truth to tell. In fact it wasn't much later that they had to chain the animal up and threaten not to recharge him if he didn't cool down. The Prof was all for switching him off for the day but the children wouldn't hear of it. It upset him too much.

All through the day the bustle went on, in a house full of weird noises. From the far-off wing where Father lived all kinds of sounds, some musical some downright dreadful, made themselves heard. There was the skirling of bag-pipes, low and mournful, then a burst of Under the Double Eagle, then a strange mixture of the two. Every now and again they heard a few bars of the Posthorn Gallop. Cynthia guessed that Father played it without noticing, when he was trying to think.

At last it was almost dusk. They were so busy they hadn't noticed the time, until the clock cuckooed seventeen times to warn them. They suddenly realised they'd have to be off.

George ran to the parents' house and asked Dad if he was ready.

'Well, lad, have a listen and tell me what you think.'

'No time, no time,' George panted. 'Come on, Pa, get your coat and scarf on. We've left it rather late.'

Cynthia and George got their father tucked into the glove compartment with his instruments while the Prof started up the Driverless Tractor. As usual, they forgot the sandwiches and flasks.

While the engine was warming up the Prof asked for directions.

As George explained the route step by step, from his memories of the day before, the Prof pressed buttons on the dashboard, turned knobs, and jiggled levers. This was why the tractor was called driverless. You fed all the information about your route into it, then it did the thinking for you. That way its legs worked for themselves, feeling the ground and getting the right grip. If you'd tried to drive it over rough ground yourself, it would have been upside-down in a jiffy, even with the hickory walking stick to help. As it was, only the Prof knew how to work the thing, it was so complicated.

Soon it was warmed up and set to go.

'Hold on tight now,' said the Prof. 'This is going to be a rough ride.'

He turned the lever to full speed and pressed the 'Go' button. With a roar the Yorkshire Moors Driverless Tractor loped out of the farmyard and onto the grassland.

They had indeed left it very late. The tractor engine ground and roared as it made its very best speed. They were banged and bounced about until they were battered and bruised.

By now the thaw was complete. Although it was nice to be quite warm again, it meant that the ground was extremely boggy, and the tractor had to strain and struggle all the time. Its boots kept getting stuck in deep muddy holes and its waterproof socks were soon covered in black, greasy slime. Time and again it had to stop in the middle of a bog and claw its way off left or right to find another route. No ordinary vehicle would have got a hundred yards.

'Oh dear oh dear,' said the Prof after a long time, 'it's very late. Will we make it before dark I wonder?'

'We've got to,' said Cynthia. 'We've *got* to!'

Just then George gave a shout.

'That's it!' he cried. 'That's the last hill! We're almost there! Make sure the tractor stops all right, Prof. We don't want to be seen.'

He needn't have worried. Just before they reached the

brow of the hill, as the Prof's hand was hovering over the 'Stop' button, the tractor lurched to a halt. Its engine switched off. A strange silence filled their ears.

'Wow,' said Cynthia. 'Thank goodness! A few more minutes of that lolloping and lurching and I think I'd have been sick!'

She wasn't the only one who felt that way. Father was a peculiar greenish colour, and the Prof could hardly stand upright when he got out of the tractor. The ground still appeared to be heaving and swaying.

'There's no time to wait and see if one of them goes out or anything like that,' said George in a trembly voice. 'It'll be pitch black in a minute or two. Oooh, I feel sick!'

Five seconds later they peered over the top of the hill. Five seconds later they felt even sicker.

There below them was the crossroads. There beside it was the lay-by.

But in the lay-by there was nothing. The caravan had gone.

CHAPTER FOURTEEN

The Hunting of the Snark

It was a very tired and miserable party that got back to the house several hours later. Father – he got weary very quickly now that he was so small – was packed off to bed so that the others could have a conference to try to decide what to do.

They had searched for as long as it was humanly possible, both in the tractor and out of it. The lay-by held no clues. Not a scrap of rubbish, not a piece of paper, not even any clear tyre-tracks. They'd walked round and round in bigger and bigger circles in the hope that the spies had just gone over a brow and hidden. But they hadn't. There was nothing. And in the dark, on the soggy, boggy moors, it had really been a waste of time from the first. Only no one would admit it.

'But why?' said Cynthia sadly. 'That's what I can't understand. Why have they gone? It's daft.'

'Unless,' the Prof added grimly, 'George got the message wrong. You didn't, did you, George?'

Even Cynthia was prepared to admit that that hadn't happened.

'Don't be daft, Prof,' she said. 'You know George doesn't get things like that wrong. He's too practical.'

George nodded.

'Not a chance I'm afraid, Prof. They said we were to be there by tonight with the machine. No machine, no Mother.'

The Prof sighed.

'Maybe we were too early.'

'Oh rubbish,' Cynthia said. 'We hung about for hours. They've gone and that's that. But *why*, I wonder.'

'And where, even more important,' George added.

'And what are we going to do?' said the Prof.

When it came down to it there was only one thing they could do. But Cynthia, red in the face with shame, admitted that they probably wouldn't get much help from that quarter.

Sure enough, when they trooped into the sitting room and the Prof gently uncovered it, the Thinks Computer made it quite clear that they'd come to the wrong place if they wanted advice.

After flashing and humming like a swarm of bees gone crazy, it came out with this message:

> There once was an idiot called Cynthia,
> Whose boots were too small for her feet.
> I told her I wanted to help her
> And she covered me up with a sheet.
> Well you've made your bed now so just lie on it,
> You'll get less than nothing from me;
> And remember in future that wisdom comes dear,
> But good manners, dear Cynthia, are free.

The light came on for the end of the message. The Prof tried again, with apologies, with flannel, with everything he could think of. Cynthia left the room to have a cry. But nothing else came. The Thinks Computer just sat there, flickering moodily.

In the kitchen again George patted her on the head.

'Never mind, love,' he said. 'It's a stupid bossy thing. It didn't really have anything sensible to say this afternoon. It was just trying it on.'

Cynthia sniffled and tried to smile.

'It's so hard living with these nutty inventions some-times, Prof,' she said. 'I do wish we could be like other people. But I am sorry about annoying the computer. Really I am.'

Before the Prof could reply the telephone started to ring. Cynthia braved the unfriendly flickering of the Thinks Computer to gather round with the other two. The Prof picked up the receiver.

'Hullo,' he said nervously (they didn't get many telephone calls), 'It's the Prof here.'

They all almost collapsed at the voice that boomed out. It was a spy!

'Haha!' it said. 'Ve are having a message for you and ze two leedle bratlings. Ve are very very angry. You may never see ze leedle mother again!'

'Gosh you leave our mum alone, you big bully!' George shouted. 'If I get hold of you you'll know something!'

A deep and horrible laugh came from the phone.

'Hello, is zat you, Georgie? Hah, my boy, you haf me tremblink like ze tea-leaf! Wiz brains like yours, how vill you ever catch me, heh? Ho, by ze vay, thank you for your mother. A useful present!'

Cynthia, for once, was more practical than George.

'Never mind all that,' she yelled. 'Where are you? Why weren't you there? We waited for ages.'

There was a short pause.

Then: 'Hhm. Vell, zat is ze good question. I vill be tellink you.' The voice suddenly went very high and angry. 'Zat voman! She is driving us mad! She negs negs negs! She negged us so much ve vere having to leave ze caravan and get in ze Rover! And ve vere so cold ve vere having to drive around to keep ze heater going. Ve have ze breakdown on ze moor and are spending tens of pounds to getting goink again. Ve are stuck in some awful place and ve must sleep in ze Rover. She negs!'

They looked at each other.

'Oh dear,' said the Prof. 'It wasn't just us, then . . .'

'Have you tried ice?' George asked the voice. 'It works wonders.'

'Leesen, Georgie,' said the voice nastily. 'There is something a lot better zan ice to keep someone quiet. Are you understandink? To keep zem quiet for good!'

All their mouths dropped open in horror.

'You couldn't!' whispered Cynthia. 'Not our mum!'

'Ho no? Ve'll be seeink about zat.'

'What do you want us to do,' George said quickly. 'We'll do anything. But we've got the machine remember. Harm one hair on her head and you'll never get even a sniff of it. *And* you'll go to prison. Tell us where to meet you and you can have it. But hurry!'

Another pause.

'All right,' said the voice. 'Ve might still do ze deal. But ve are very very angry. Charlie is all for lettink you stew in ze juices. I hef to make him change his mind. So you must vait see. Zat is all. You must vait, and vorry, and vorry and vait. And maybe ve phones you and maybe ve don'ts. You must vait. All right?'

What could they say?

'And just think of zis to keep you heppy. She negs us like ze madvoman. If she isn't stoppink, ve might do like I said, huh?'

'You pig!' screamed Cynthia.

But the phone had gone dead.

They sat round the kitchen table more worried and gloomy than they'd ever been. Now they were in terrible trouble. The men had gone, Mother was nagging herself into an early grave if she wasn't careful, they'd no idea where the spies were or if they'd ever be in touch again. It was dreadful.

It was also an odd time for the Snark to start getting playful. But he did. They ignored him, they shouted at him, they threatened to switch him off. But he carried on nipping their ankles and performing weird antics on the flagstones.

At last George said: 'I think the daft dog's trying to tell us something.'

The Snark barked joyfully, wagging his tail.

'By George you're right, George,' said the Prof. 'Oh well, no harm in watching, I suppose.'

The Snark went through a most peculiar series of actions. He jumped on to his back legs, fell over with his paws clutched across his stomach, made howling noises as though he'd been kicked. Then he got up and sniffed and snuffled loudly through his nose, darting here and there all round the kitchen. Everyone was baffled.

'Sorry, old Snark,' said George at last. 'We don't know what you're up to. It looks like charades.'

Again the Snark leaped about, barking joyfully.

'It *is* charades?' asked George.

The Snark actually nodded his head.

'Charades!' said Cynthia, excited. She was good at charades. 'Do it again, Snarkie, go on.'

Again the dog fell over backwards, this time with a single bark.

'Sounds as though he's been shot,' said the Prof. Joyful barks.

'Simple in that case,' said Cynthia. 'Let's try some shot-type charade words. Gun? Bullet? Explosion? Hurt? Dead? Blood?'

The Snark went wild.

'Blood!' said Cynthia.

'What does that mean?' said George.

The Snark went into his sniffing routine. He did it three times, till Cynthia stopped him.

'I've got it, Snarkie,' she said. 'You . . . are . . . a . . . BLOODHOUND!'

He rolled over to have his belly scratched. If dogs could smile the Snark would have cracked his jaw.

'Jolly good,' said the Prof sourly. 'So the Snark's cleverer than we thought. He can play charades.'

'Oh you silly old twit,' said Cynthia rudely. 'Not just charades. Don't you see? He can play bloodhounds too!'

The penny dropped.

'You mean? You're saying? Good golly gosh, of course! He goes for the paper, he wanders the moors. He never gets lost! Well I'm blessed! What a fantastic dog!'

The Snark's happiness was complete.

After that they all had a cup of snooze, as it was too late for anything other than a good night's sleep. In the morning Cynthia and George got on boots over their Thermals, made more coffee and sandwiches, which they forgot of course, and set off on the long walk to the lay-by to pick up the trail.

The Prof stayed at home in case the spies phoned. In any event he was too old for heavy work like this. Father they didn't even tell. He had enough to worry about already. The children and their dog were excited and happy. They'd find the spies' hideout, report back, and the attack could go on as planned.

But it was a pity the Snark wasn't a real bloodhound.

Or he might have picked up an interesting scent very close to the house.

Very close indeed.

CHAPTER FIFTEEN

Total Disaster

Almost as soon as they reached the lay-by the Snark was on to something. Strangely enough, in daylight, there were plenty of signs that the spies had been there. There was quite a large amount of rubbish lying around, not even in the bins. To George and Cynthia, who lived on the moors and hated people who dropped garbage and litter, it was the final evidence that the spies were bad men. They held an old tea-cloth with a strong pong to the Snark's nostrils, then said 'Seek, boy, seek'. (As though it hadn't been his idea in the first place!)

The dog ran round and round the lay-by about five times, then moved out into the road. Luckily there was no traffic at all, as the Snark followed the course of the Land Rover and caravan exactly. He kept up a cracking pace. Soon Cynthia and George were blowing out clouds of steam into the cold early morning air.

At first the spies seemed not to have been able to make up their minds. Or perhaps they were making sure anyone trying to track them would have a hard job of it. Several times the Snark went off the road onto the edge of the moors, did a couple of big circles, got on the tarmac once more, then set off in the opposite direction. When they passed the lay-by for the third time, both children were getting short of breath – and temper.

'They were up to something all right,' George panted. 'Either that or they're barmy.'

'And I'm pretty sure they're not that,' Cynthia puffed

back. 'They must have guessed what we'd do even before we decided to do it!'

'We!' wheezed George. 'If it had been left to us we'd still be sitting at home moping.'

This time the Snark took the fourth road from the crossroads, and at last settled down to a bit of straight-forward running. They kept up an easy loping pace, helped by the fact that the moor was sloping downhill on this road. Soon they hit a village and George called a halt so that they could 'borrow' a drink of water from a cafe.

'Gosh,' said Cynthia, 'I couldn't half use a glass of lemonade.'

But it was out of the question. The only money they had was for the telephone in case they found something.

They asked the cafe man if he'd seen the Land Rover and the caravan, but he said he hadn't. George was inclined to get worried, but the Snark was waiting impatiently when they came outside, and set off without them telling him to. The trail was obviously very hot.

Later on, when they passed through the third or fourth village, things were getting more difficult. As the day got older the traffic got heavier. Apart from having to leap into the ditch every now and again to avoid being squashed, the Snark was finding the scent more and more covered by all the petrol fumes and tracks of the other cars and lorries. When they reached a small town with several roads off

from the centre he wandered around for a good long time, sniffing hard. His tail had stopped wagging, too.

A bent old fellow in a tweed overcoat and cap, sitting under the war memorial, watched them for a few minutes. Then he waved his stick and shouted them over.

'Ee there's been some goings on here this morning,' he said. 'All the queer folk in Yorkshire seem to have come in. Not even market day, neither.'

'Queer folk?' said George. 'What sort of queer folk?'

'You'll not believe this even if I tell thee,' said the old fellow. 'But I'll tell thee just same. Ey up, though, what sort of a dog's that yon?'

Cynthia laughed.

'You'd not believe us if we told thee,' she said. 'But we'll tell thee just same. It's electric.'

'Ah,' said the old fellow. 'Pull the other one lass, it's got bells on!'   He roared with laughter, waving his stick in the air. Tears ran down his cheeks.

'You're a funny quiet pair, though,' he said at last. 'Electric dog! Ah, I like that!'

George coughed politely.

'What sort of queer folk please, sir?' he asked timidly. 'We're . . . er . . . we're looking for some actually. Some *very* queer folk.'

'Oh aye, well 'appen you've come to right place,' said the old fellow. 'How about the fattest man in t'world, eh? Will he do for a start?'

'Hooray!' George shouted. 'Have you seen him? Did he have—'

'Ey up, young fellow,' said the old man. 'Who's telling this tale, thee or me? You'd not believe the one 'e 'ad with him. He were—'

'Big and ugly with a bristly chin and a crew cut,' said Cynthia. 'And they were driving a jeep with a caravan behind it. Which way did they go?'

The old fellow looked put out. They'd spoiled his story. George smiled politely.

'Please,' he said.

The old man smiled too.

'Ah well,' he said. 'I suppose nowt's strange to young folk nowadays.' He pointed with his stick. 'They went that road. Up over toward Oldham way. Asked me the way did the fat one. Reet funny voice. Foreign.' He shook his head, laughing. 'Ey, but he were fat, though!'

Even Cynth had the sense to shout 'Thank you'. They chased the Snark up the right road at top speed. When they were a few hundred yards from the town centre he picked up the trail again, barking madly.

By lunchtime they were in another town, dying of starvation and again stuck for a trail. As they passed a fish and chip shop they dribbled. George got quite ratty with Cynthia, he was so hungry.

'You are a fool, Cynth,' he snapped. 'You always forget the sandwiches. You'll forget your head next!'

'Me!' she shouted. 'You cheeky pig, George. It was you who forgot the sandwiches. *I* was in charge of the coffee!'

'Hhm,' George muttered sulkily. 'Well a drink would've been a help!'

They stood outside the chippy with their tongues hanging out. The Snark was up to his old trick of running around in frantic circles trying to find which way the spies had gone. After a while the chippy man, a big, sad-looking fellow, came to the door.

'What's trouble, kids?' he said, in a big sad voice. 'Got no money?'

They nodded.

'Ee, I'm a fool,' he said. 'I'll end up in poorhouse, I will.'

He scooped two bags of chips out, put on tons of salt and vinegar, and handed them over. They said thank you nicely. George offered him a chip.

'No thanks, son,' he said. 'Never touch 'em meself. Nasty fattening things. Ee, they're going down, though. Proper hungry you must have been.'

'We were,' said Cynthia with her mouth full. 'We're hunting two spies. They've kidnapped our mum.'

'Oh aye,' said Sam (that was his name). ''Appen I've seen 'em. Big fellow who needs a shave and a little fat chap. Right little butterbarrel.'

The children gaped.

'Strangest order I've ever 'ad,' Sam added. 'Fish and chips twice and one large chip cut up small with a razor blade. Barmy.'

The children gasped.

'Which way did they go?' said George. 'That's them!'

Sam pointed to a high narrow road leading up the moor that rose behind the town.

'Straight up there,' he said. 'And if you ever find them you might tell the fat one I'll push his face in if he comes here again. He gave me a foreign coin!'

Full of hot free chips they made good time up the road. It was hardly ever used and the trail was singing in the Snark's nostrils. When the town was well out of sight he turned left off the road and bounded across the grass. Two hundred yards later the ground got boggy. There, as clear as daylight for all to see, were the deep tyre tracks of a Land Rover and caravan. The children whooped.

So excited were they by the easy trail, so fast were they clambering over the difficult ground, that it wasn't for some time that Cynthia stopped with a piercing shriek.

'George!' she yelled. 'Look where we are! Just look!'

He looked, panting. Just a stretch of moorland like any other. Wild, bleak, windy and wet.

Just like any other? Not a bit of it! He knew that peak! He knew that funny-shaped pile of rock on the horizon.

'Blimey!' he squawked. 'We're almost home!'

As they stood in silent horror, a strange, lonely noise came wafting towards them over the brow.

'Oh no,' George whispered. 'Listen, Cynth! Oh listen!'

It was the faint skirling of bagpipes. They were playing Amazing Grace.

The children put their heads down and raced up the hill till the blood hammered in their ears. But when they got to the top, they knew they were too late.

Down below them lay the house. Outside it stood the Rover and the caravan. They all looked like toys, about half a mile away.

As they watched, the sound of the bagpipes stopped abruptly. The Snark whined and George seized his collar. A few seconds later three people came out of the house. One fat, one big – and the Prof. He was carefully carrying a bag, which they guessed had Father in it. Balanced on his shoulder the big spy, Mrs Ponsonby-Smythe, had the shrinking machine.

'We've got to stop them!' cried Cynthia. 'Come on, George, run!'

'Ssssh! Be quiet,' he said softly. 'And keep still. Cynthia, we've got one chance and one chance only. We've got to stay free.'

He pulled her behind a clump of heather.

'Keep hidden until they've gone,' he added. 'It's the only way.'

CHAPTER SIXTEEN

Cheap Day Return

As Cynthia and George watched the caravan lurch and lumber slowly out of sight they felt terrible. But when they walked through the kitchen door, which was lolloping on one hinge, they felt a million times worse. The house was a complete disaster area. It was as though a bomb had hit it. The kitchen table was upsidedown, the cuckoo was hanging limp on its spring from out of its gaily-painted doors, two chairs were broken. It was awful.

'Gosh,' said Cynthia. 'The Prof must have put up a heck of a fight! What a mess!'

'The pigs,' said George. 'The rotten pigs! What did they have to go and break the place up for?'

The door to the inventing room was slightly open. Cynthia sniffed the air and ran over to it. George picked up the remains of his favourite mug, the one with the dragon painted on it. There was a shout.

'George! George! Quick! Put out the cat!'

He couldn't believe his ears.

'What are you talking about, you idiot!' he said.

'The cat! We've got to put it out! Help me!'

'She's gone potty,' George muttered, walking towards the door. 'Put out the cat at a time like this!'

But when he got to the inventing room Cynthia was chasing Viva round and round. And there were two thick plumes of smoke pouring from pussy's earholes.

'Grab her, George,' shrieked Cynthia. 'Put her out before she burns the place down!'

Viva made a dash between George's legs, but he clicked his ankles together.

'Ouch!' The cat was red hot.

Almost without thinking George rushed to the washing up bowl in the sink. He dunked Viva into the dirty water.

Flash! Bang! Sizzle!

With a heart-rending howl, the electronic cat stopped moving. Her tail went limp.

'Oh poor Viva,' said George. 'She's blown a fuse!'

It was almost too much for Cynthia. She cradled the lifeless cat to her chest and rocked it, crooning.

'Poor poor poor little thing,' she sang. 'What have the nasty nasty men done to you?'

'Oh shut up, Cynth, do,' snapped George. 'She always was totally unreliable, anyway. Listen, we've got important things to do.'

Cynthia chucked Viva onto the one chair which still had all four legs.

'Oh yeah, Cleverclogs,' she said. 'Like what? Go on, you just tell me. I'll be very pleased to hear. Just . . . exactly . . . *what* . . . have . . . we . . . got . . . to . . . do?'

'Well,' said George. He stopped. He put his forehead in his hand. He was stumped.

'Oh, George,' said Cynthia. 'Sometimes it's hard being a kid, isn't it? What *are* we going to do?'

George shook his head.

'We've got to get them back. All of them. Mum, Dad, the Prof, the machine. But . . . '

The Snark, which had been exploring on his own account, came out of the living room. He whined.

Cynthia looked first at the dog, then at the door. Her face lit up. She snapped her fingers.

'The Thinks Computer! Crikey, I know it's off me at the moment, but it wouldn't let us down at a time like this.'

George whooped. They ran to the door. And stopped, frozen with horror.

The Thinks Computer, the smug, bad-tempered, self-satisfied Thinks Computer, was dead. It lay beside the comfy armchair looking all wrong. It had been smashed.

They couldn't believe it. They just couldn't. They stood and wept.

'Oh, George,' said Cynthia at last. 'What *have* they done to our dear machine?'

Slowly they walked towards it. There was no sign of life. None. Nothing. Not one light flickered. Not the vaguest, faintest hint of a hum.

'The swine,' said George. 'The rotten, vicious, nasty swine.'

Because the Thinks Computer looked so sad, so damaged, they tried to get it upright again. As they strained at the dead, heavy lump they pushed the armchair to one side. Cynthia noticed something.

'George! Look! Lower it down again.'

They eased the machine to the floor and pushed the chair away. On the wall, very faint, was a message. It was a short poem, written by the computer's flexing arm, dipped in the light machine oil which dripped from its wounds.

It was hard to read, in shaky, straggly writing.

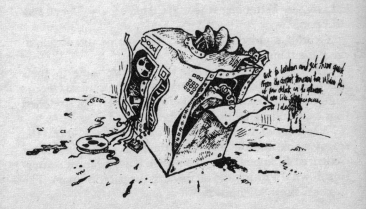

Get to London and get there quick
From the airport tomorrow these villains fly.
At four o'clock in the afternoon,
And now, like Shakespeare, I die . . . I die . . .

'Written in his own blood,'whispered Cynthia. 'How brave! And how clever to have heard their plan. I hope he forgave me before he . . . went.'

'Yuk, you're soppy!' said George. 'What do you want, a signed pardon? Come on! Let's get to London! Shakespeare my eye!'

They were halfway out of the kitchen before the thought struck them. Cynthia tapped George on the shoulder.

'How though? We've only got 10p.'

This time they were baffled. They couldn't hitch, obviously. That was out of the question for children. They couldn't phone and ask Cedric's advice, because the spies had cut off the phone. They couldn't pawn the family silver, because there was no pawnshop . . . and no silver either.

'We could try the piggy bank,' said George doubtfully.

'Oh yes,' said Cynth. 'Rather you than me, brother. Anyway, there wouldn't be enough in it.'

'Got any better ideas then? We'll have to try. Does it *have* to be me?'

Cynthia nodded. But she agreed to come and watch, to give him courage.

The piggy bank was on the dressing table in their bedroom. Cynthia stood nervously by the door as George tiptoed towards it. He got closer and closer. He stretched out his hands gingerly. Then he pounced.

A split-second later he gave a terrific yell and threw the piggy-bank into the air. It hit the floor with a bang and scuttled off, squealing blue murder. They heard it clattering down the stairs, and off towards the parents' room. The squeals slowly died away.

'Rotten stupid thing,' said George, blowing on his shocked hands. 'I'd like to kick its head in.'

'What puzzles me,' said Cynthia, as they moped back to the kitchen, 'is how it knows. You never get an electric shock if you go to put something *in*!'

'Like everything else in this madhouse,' said George. 'Oh, Cynth, I wish we were normal!'

There was only one thing left and they both knew it. They didn't mention it for a long time, though, because they didn't really want to think about it. Anyway, they both knew what Cynthia would say when George brought it up.

At last they could wait no longer.

'There's only one thing for it, old girl,' said George. 'The cheap day return transferer.'

She stuck out her chin stubbornly.

'No, no, no, no, a thousand million times *no*!' she said. 'George I will do *anything* except go in that crazy machine.'

The argument was long and difficult. The cheap day return transferer summed up just about everything Cynthia hated about science and inventions. She thought it was unnecessary, dangerous, ridiculous. George agreed secretly. But just at the moment he couldn't say so.

Twenty five minutes later they opened the door to the old railway carriage in the yard, asked for two returns to London – half fare – at the automatic ticket office, and sat themselves nervously in a musty, dusty, fusty old compartment. It was dark and cold, with drawn blinds and a dim electric bulb in the ceiling. George and Cynthia held hands and waited for the train to start. Their eyes were tightly shut.

CHAPTER SEVENTEEN

The Emergency Chest

The carriage, which had once belonged to a little branch line that ran out onto the moors from Lancashire to Yorkshire, was a very ramshackle affair of wood and leather and fat, dust-filled seats. As soon as they'd got themselves settled there was a whistle, a jerk and a smooth, swaying motion. All the sounds of an old-fashioned station filled their ears, along with the puffing of a wheezy little steam locomotive. Although the Prof's invention was bang up-to-date, the gear he'd made it from was from bygone days.

At first the easy, gentle motion was soothing. After a couple of minutes they opened their eyes. It wasn't so scary after all. The little old engine puffed away up front, and the carriage picked up speed until it was rocking along very comfortably.

'Hey,' said Cynthia. 'This isn't so bad at all. Shall we have the blinds up?'

'Why not,' said George. 'I told you we'd be all right, didn't I?'

Strangely, the view when they could see out was not what they expected. They were running through a flat land, with fields stretching out for a long way. It wasn't the moors.

'How odd,' said Cynthia. 'It seems to have shifted us to a different place.'

'Yes,' said George, 'well I suppose it would, wouldn't it? I mean, we're going to London, aren't we?'

They watched the scenery slip by without a word for quite a long time. Almost without them noticing it, the train was getting faster. The telegraph poles began to flash by and the coach began to sway.

All at once they passed a level-crossing. At the gates there were two or three vintage motor cars waiting. And a traction-engine. And a huge cartload of hay – being drawn by two horses.

'Did you see what I saw?' asked Cynthia. She took George's hand again.

He gave a nervous laugh.

'Old car rally,' he said. 'And traction engines. People collect them, you know.'

Soon they were being rocked from side to side. The telegraph poles were getting blurred. The puffing of the engine was now a steady roar.

'George?' asked Cynthia, as they rattled over some points with a tremendous clattering, 'don't you think this train's going rather fast?'

George laughed again. But it was even more nervous this time.

'Well we've got a long way to go. The Prof says you can get from anywhere to anywhere in a few minutes.' He paused. 'That's the idea, anyway.'

'Oh dear,' said Cynthia.

'You see,' George went on, 'when we arrive in London, our watches will say it's only a little while since we left. The Snark went from the house to Macclesfield and back in one and half minutes.'

'And came back covered in seaweed,' said Cynthia. 'Oh George, I wish we hadn't.'

A station went by – or rather they went through a station. But by now they were going so fast that they hardly glimpsed the buildings, let alone the nameplate. The din was terrific; battering of wheels on rails, roaring of wind, the hammering of the locomotive.

Suddenly there was darkness for a split second.

'What was that?' squeaked Cynthia.

'A tunnel,' said George. His voice was shaking. 'Cynthia we went through that tunnel in a flash. Unless it was only one foot long we must be doing hundreds of miles an hour!'

Five minutes later it got dark again. Not so suddenly. It took half a minute. Then they saw stars. Actual stars, hurrying through the black sky.

'George, it's *night*!' yelled Cynthia. 'It's gone night-time!'

And less than ten minutes later, dawn broke. Now even the fields were a frightening, whizzing blur.

Cynthia's voice became very firm.

'George,' she said. 'Press the abort button.'

This was a device that the Prof had built in after the early experiments. He didn't know exactly what its effect would be, but he hoped . . .

'Hey – we're slowing down,' said George.

There was a long, agonised howling of brakes. The compartment shuddered and vibrated. As they got slower, night fell again, still much quicker than normal. By the time they stopped it was pitch black. A man walked along the platform towards them, carrying a lamp. It was an oil lamp.

George pulled down the window by its leather strap and leaned out.

'Excuse me,' he yelled. 'Is this London?'

The man walked very, very slowly towards them. The locomotive hissed and clanked in the cold night air.

'Excuse me,' George said again, quietly. 'Is this London?'

Slowly, very slowly, the man lifted the lamp till the light shone on his face. It was horribly old, and dead white, and his eyes were deep and red and shiny. As George watched in horror he reached out a thin, bony hand with long curved nails towards the carriage door.

'London, young sir?' he said. His voice was cold, and old, and sort of slimy. 'Oh dear no, this ain't London. The London line won't be finished till 1847. This is called Devil's Halt. And it's the end of the line. For both of you!'

The second before his finger touched the handle, Cynthia's punched the abort button. The world span. There was a screaming, roaring, howling noise. The carriage shook and bounced and flung them from side to side. Over and over and over it spun, like a vast tumble-drier. The two children were knocked about, trying to hold on to things and to each other. It was awful.

Then – silence. The compartment became still. There was nothing. No engine noise. No station noise. Just a faint whining of wind outside.

Cynthia and George got up off the floor and looked through the window, wondering what dreadful thing they'd see next. To their eternal relief, it was their own backyard.

When they got into the kitchen, the Snark went wild with joy. They'd tried to get him to come with them, rather than leave him all alone in the house, but he had simply refused to be caught. One trip to Macclesfield was enough for that wise animal. From the way he carried on he'd obviously thought he'd never see them again once they entered the transferer.

It soon became clear, though, that while they'd been gone he'd had another brainwave. He tugged at the bottoms of their Thermals until they followed him out of the house.

The dog trotted ahead, barking and looking over his shoulder, until they came to one of the disused pit shafts nearby. This was from the days when coal was mined in the area. There were quite a few of them, and the children avoided them like the plague, because they were so dangerous. They stood at the head of the shaft, with the Snark wagging its tail and whining, wondering what they were meant to do next.

'What's he on about, I wonder,' said George. 'Why's he brought us to the pit shaft?'

The answer came to Cynthia like a blinding light.

'The emergency chest!' she shrieked. 'Oh, Snarkie! You *clever* boy!'

The Snark rolled onto his back and she gave him a tickle. George looked doubtful.

'Blimey, Cynth,' he said. 'The emergency chest? That's *strictly* for grown-ups. Do you think we ought?'

The Snark barked. Yes!

Cynthia smiled.

'I know it's terrible, George. But crikey. If *this* isn't an emergency, just what the heck *is*?'

The rules about the emergency chest were simple. It was the last resort. The final thing. To be gone to when all else had failed. It was *not* for children. In fact the children weren't even meant to know it existed. Nor where it was hidden. But they did, of course, being nosy little devils. And a jolly good thing too!

Quickly they got a rope from the barn and pulled away some planks covering the shaft. George tied a good knot and prepared to take the strain. Cynthia was going down, because she was a better climber, and because George was actually a bit scared of heights. She called up every time she needed more rope paying out. It seemed quite a long time before she shouted 'Got it!'

Down in the old shaft it was horrible. It was pitch black and very dank and chill. Cynthia had no idea how far down it went, but when she knocked off a small piece of rock it was ages and ages and ages before she heard it reach the bottom. And it made a splash. She shivered. Hundreds of feet down into black, cold hideous water.

There were noises too. Groanings and creaks, like very old ghosts sighing. Cynthia trembled as she stuffed the box into her knapsack and started to climb up again. She was terrified.

As they looked at the dirty little box lying on the kitchen table they were both even more terrified. It was one of the Prof's ideas, which meant they could find *anything* in it. They didn't really want to open it. But they had to.

George got a cloth and wiped the lid. It had something written on it – burnt in with a hot poker.

It said:

WARNING – EMERGENCY CHEST
'This box contains the most dangerous thing known to man. If used with *extreme* care it can sometimes be a help.'
BUT DON'T COUNT ON IT!

'Oh crumbs,' said Cynthia. 'Whatever can it be?'

George gritted his teeth and pulled back the two catches. He opened the lid. Inside there was a sheet of paper which said: 'You have been warned!'

And underneath that, there were four five-pound notes.

CHAPTER EIGHTEEN

Two Sorts of Help

By the time they reached the farmless farmhouse in Mill Hill next morning, Cedric and Mabel had gone to work and Jugears and Mophead were at school. But they weren't too worried, because luckily the boys had already shown them what the family called the 'burglar's entrance'. They went round the back of the house to where some overgrown bushes covered what used to be the coalhole before the heating was put in. Two minutes later they were inside, a bit coaldusty but all right. Dougal the faithful watchdog didn't even wake up until the Snark gave him a playful nip!

That playful nip had a bad effect though. Dougal was so pleased to see them, and so delighted to have the Snark to play with, that the two dogs started barking and tearing about. Then there was silence. Next moment George saw them racing off down the street, trailing coaldust. He rushed to the front door and shouted at them, but they took no notice.

'Hey, that's the last thing we need,' he said. 'Fancy that stupid Snark doing a thing like that.'

'Never mind that now,' replied Cynthia. 'Let's just get on the phone to the Government and tell them what's happened. We haven't got much time.'

George took the phone in the hall and Cynthia listened in from Cedric and Mabel's bedroom. The Government's number was scrawled on the front of the telephone book – the Prof was an untidy sort of man – so there was no difficulty there.

But oh, the difficulty once they'd got through to the Houses of Parliament! The humming and hahing, the switching from person to person, the passing of the buck.

In a pause as they were switched for the umpteenth time, Cynthia sighed: 'It's amazing how people go on, George. They must spend all their lives trying to avoid doing anything.'

'Yeah,' said George. 'This time we actually know who to ask for. And *still* we can't get him.'

Just as if to prove him wrong there was a click and a voice said: 'Minister of Extremely Secret Things speaking. Who is it?'

George cleared his throat and put on his deepest voice.

'Ah good morning, Mr Minister,' he said. 'You may remember me. I have something very very important to discuss with you.'

When the Minister guessed who it was he almost put the phone down. But George managed to stop him by mentioning spies. Very keen on spies, was the Minister.

Cynthia cut in: 'Mrs Ponsonby-Smythe, sir? Remember her? I bet she doesn't work for you any more!'

The Minister coughed nervously.

'I cannot discuss Government business with the likes of you, young lady,' he said.

'Yah!' said Cynthia. 'I bet she doesn't, though, does she!'

'Well,' said the Minister. 'I suppose I'd better listen to you. Although after your disgusting behaviour last time we met I could have you shot or locked up. I hope you realise that.'

George apologised most humbly, while Cynthia stuck her tongue out at the phone but said nothing. The Minister listened in silence as George told the tale. Of the kidnapping, the hunt for the spies, and the final disaster.

'Hm,' he said at last. 'And one of them was Mrs Ponsonby-Smythe, you say? Never did trust that woman, you know. Shouldn't be surprised if he wasn't a Johnny-Foreigner, what?'

'Of course he was foreign!' shrieked Cynthia. 'He's a spy! You're so—'

'Cynthia!' George shouted. 'Remember your manners, you idiot.'

This time Cynthia apologised. The Minister's voice got positively warm.

'Well, children,' he said. 'It certainly is an amusing little tale. Yes. Well, I've taken a lot of notes. Give me a few days to think it over and I'll see if there's anything to be done.'

The children couldn't believe their ears.

'Days?' whispered George. 'You can't be serious?'

'But why not?' replied the Minister, surprised. 'In the business of good government one cannot afford to be hasty. Anything could happen. Look before you leap is our motto.'

'I'm awfully sorry to bother you,' George said. 'But days would really be too late. I mean, we've been told that the spies are flying out today.'

'And who told you that pray?'

'Well it was the Thinks Computer actually. It was its dying message. It wrote it on the wall.'

'In its life's blood,' added Cynthia fiercely.

The Minister laughed.

'Ah yes, children, very funny. Haha, very funny indeed. A computer that thinks and writes messages in blood. Oh, you are a caution!'

'But it's *true*,' said George desperately. 'At least check up that there's a flight at 4 o'clock. They'll be on it. We'll lose our parents!'

'Oh yes, there's a flight at four o'clock all right,' the Minister replied chirpily. 'I know all the flight-times to the places spies are likely to go!'

'Well,' said George. 'What are you going to do? Will you stop them?'

'My dear child,' said the Minister irritably. 'I've told you what I'll do. I'll think it over. I'll sleep on it.'

Cynthia groaned. Some people were so *stupid*.

George tried lying, but he wasn't very good at it.

'The machine,' he mumbled. 'You know, the shrinker. Well, it's finished. The Prof's got it going right. It's a weapon of great stratee . . . stratee . . . it's very super. I mean, any Government in their right mind . . . '

'I don't wish to be rude,' said the Minister, 'but monkey nuts to that. I hope you get my meaning?'

'But the parents. The Prof. What's going to happen to them?'

George's voice was so trembly that the Minister got kindly.

'Never mind, little boy,' he said. 'There is one thing you seem to have forgotten. The Customs. They are always on guard, you know. They have eyes like hawks. It would be impossible to smuggle a rubber duck out of this country, let alone a Professor with a shrinking machine that doesn't work and two six-inch high dolls.'

Cynthia screamed at him: 'They are *not* dolls! They are our mummy and daddy! And it *does* work, you silly politician!'

'Yes yes,' said the Minister. 'Well don't bust a button, little girl. The Customs will stop them.'

'Couldn't you at least warn them?' asked George. 'Tell the Customs what to look out for?'

'Good golly no!' said the Minister. 'They wouldn't like that at all! They might think I was criticising. Well, goodbye now. Oh, and by the way – good luck!'

With a last friendly chuckle he put down the phone. This time the children did weep. They sat on the sofa in the front room and bawled their eyes out.

They were still crying buckets when they realised someone else was in the room. Jugears and Mophead, covered with coaldust, were standing in front of them, staring in wonder. Jugears was in muddy football gear,

Mophead in ordinary school clothes. The children snuffled and sniffled and dried their eyes.

'I thought something must be up when I saw the Snark,' said Jugears. 'I was on the field. I was just going to score too. I missed scoring a goal to come and see what was up.'

'Oh isn't he the little angel!' said Mophead. '*I'll* get into worse trouble! I had to run out of the classroom when he waved!'

'Rubbish!' said Jugears. 'They won't even miss you, you're so thick. But old Fred'll kill me. I'm the best player in the school!'

The argument could have turned into a fight, but Jugears remembered George and Cynthia. They'd stopped crying, and were goggling red-eyed at the peculiar Londoners.

'Did you truly come to help?' said Cynthia. 'Oh thank you! We're in terrible trouble!'

'Course I did,' said the boys both together. 'What's the matter?'

George and Cynthia explained the whole story, in scrambled, hurried, jumbled-up sentences. Jugears and Mophead listened quietly, with their mouths hanging open.

'Wow!' said Mophead at last. 'No wonder it was meant to be a secret. If I'd put that in my daily topic there'd have been trouble!'

'Never mind secrets,' said Cynthia. 'We wanted to tell you all along. The point is, what are we going to do?'

'We've got to stop them, we've got to,' George added. 'But how? How?'

Jugears thought for a minute.

'Whenever Mabel and Cedric have a problem,' he said, 'they discuss it over a drink. I've got some some pop upstairs. Hang on a sec.'

Two minutes later they were all swigging orangeade from the bottle. George and Cynthia were beginning to feel a lot better.

After her third gulp Cynthia said: 'You will help us, won't you? Jugears? Mophead?'

'Help you!' cried the boys. 'You bet your boots we will!'

The Snark came through the front room door with Dougal. They stood and wagged their tails.

CHAPTER NINETEEN

At the Airport

Jugears and Mophead, it turned out, were pretty good at getting things going. First of all, they agreed, they'd have to do the job themselves. Absolutely no point at all in trusting to grown-ups. Which meant, Jugears pointed out, that they'd have to get to London Airport in double-quick time.

'What about the Customs?' said Cynthia. 'The Minister said they'd grab the spies.'

'Rubbish,' said Mophead. 'Don't trust 'em, Cynth. If a job needs doing well – do it yourself.'

'But how are we going to get there,' asked George. 'It's miles away, isn't it? I mean, London Airport's not actually in London, is it?'

Jugears grinned.

'Get a cab,' he said simply. 'Mabel always does.'

'A cab?' said George.

The two boys were amazed.

'A cab! You know what a *cab* is, surely? One of those big black things with a clock and a grumpy driver.'

Cynthia nudged George secretly.

'They mean a taxi,' she whispered.

'But we've got no money left,' George said. 'We had twenty pounds, but we bought a sandwich and a glass of lemonade on the train. That only left enough for the fares out here.'

Cynthia looked glum.

'How far is it?' she asked.

'Oh, about ten miles, I think,' said Mophead. 'I don't

know exactly, you never notice in a cab. Anyway, let's get going.'

'But how?' said George. 'I told you, we've got no money.'

'Pockets!' Jugears ordered Mophead. His younger brother turned them out.

'17p,' he said.

Jugears had left his pockets at school.

'All right,' he said. 'You take Cedric and Mabel's room, I'll do the lounge.'

As they went out he said to George: 'There's a piggy bank in the playroom. Get a knife from the kitchen and have a go at it, will you?'

George and Cynthia approached the piggy bank a bit fearfully. But of course, they needn't have worried. It was china, and spotted, and fat, and normal. George put his hand on it. No shock. No squeak. No nothing.

'How lovely,' he breathed. 'An actual piggy bank!'

They got more and more amazed as the money kept coming out. Fifty pence pieces, tens, fives. There wasn't a copper coin to be seen.

'Cripes,' said Cynthia. 'Where do these kids get all their pocket money from? I bet *they* don't have a punishment book!'

A few minutes later Jugears called them all together in the front room. They did a count-up of everything they'd found.

'Seven pounds sixty-two and a half,' he announced. 'That should get us there all right.'

'What about getting back?' asked Cynthia timidly.

Jugears smiled a grim smile.

'If we rescue those parents and the Prof,' he said, 'there's no problem. If we don't . . . '

'We won't *need* to get back, will we?' said Mophead.

George and Cynthia looked blank.

'Death or glory!' he hissed. 'Agreed?'

Their jaws dropped open.

'Yes,' they said. 'Death or glory!'

While Mophead phoned for a taxi, Jugears eyed Cynthia and George up and down.

'It's no good,' he said. 'You'll never get by in those baby clothes. You'll have to change them.'

George went red.

'They're not baby clothes,' he said. 'I've told you before. They're Yorkshire Moors Winter Thermals.'

'Yes, yes,' said Jugears. 'Well whatever you call them they look daft. You can't go like that.'

'Well what do you suggest?' asked Cynthia. 'We've not got anything else. What can we do?'

'I know!' said Jugears. 'How about football strip? We've not got no girls' clothes anyway. But if we all go as footballers! How about that?'

It sounded great. George bagged Manchester United again, and Cynthia decided on Stoke City. She told Jugears he really must get Oldham Athletic sometime. When Mophead came back from the phone they told him the plan.

'You're all barmy!' he said. 'I mean, those baby clothes look daft enough. But football gear! People'll think we're mad!'

It was a thought. They racked their brains.

'Got it!' said Jugears, snapping his fingers. 'We'll take a ball too!'

They all rooted out the gear, Mophead as well. But before they had time to put it on the doorbell went.

'Come on,' said Jugears. 'We'll change in the cab.'

The taxi-driver looked surprised when the strange crew of children stormed out of the farmhouse, but Jugears showed him the fistful of notes and he let them in. The two dogs bounded and snapped at each other as they waited to be pulled on board.

During the long drive they got changed easily, tying their ordinary clothes in a bundle with a piece of string from Mophead's pocket. The taxi-driver kept looking over his shoulder as though he thought they were nuts, but he didn't tell them off.

It was a long way to the airport, and the traffic was bad. Bits of the North Circular were being dug up, and at one point a lorry had skidded across a junction. The children's excited chat cooled down as the hands of their watches crept towards danger point.

'Can't we ask him to go faster?' Cynthia hissed.

'Don't be potty!' said Mophead. 'He'd chuck us out and make us walk.'

By the time they'd got to the airport and paid off the taxi, not forgetting a tip, it was frighteningly late. George and Cynthia were confused by the noise and the bustle and the excitement. The brothers grabbed them by the hands and hurried them through the crowds.

'Where are we going?' panted George. 'Where are you taking us now?'

'We'll go up to the observation platform,' Jugears said. 'See if we can spot the plane. They won't let us through the barriers anyway.'

All the time as they hurried and scuttled along, people kept staring and pointing at them. A couple of big men in uniforms wanted them to stop but they dashed onwards, the dogs at their heels.

When they got to the observation lounge they tore straight through and out onto the balcony. It was a fine day, though chilly, and there were a couple of dozen other people looking out over the vast airfield.

George and Cynthia were astonished by the size and differentness of it all. They'd have just stared at everything. They'd never seen anything like it. But Jugears and Mophead, who'd flown to Spain a couple of times, were searching for something which would tell them which plane was theirs.

It was the Snark, however, who solved the mystery. He set up a frantic barking and rested his paws on the parapet of the balcony.

George knelt beside him and looked along the electronic dog's snout. Coming out of one of the big airport buildings he saw two sinister, familiar figures.

'It's them,' he shouted. 'Cynthia! Jugmop! Headears! I mean – oh look! It's the spies!'

Out of the Customs building they walked. The shortest, fattest, nastiest man in the world and Mrs Charlie Ponsonby-Smythe. This one, big and strong, was carrying a funny-shaped parcel over his left shoulder, and pushing a long, narrow suitcase-on-wheels in front of him. Mr Fixit was carrying something the size of a small birdcage. It had breathing holes punched in the sides.

'Just look at that,' said Cynthia. 'That'll be the parents in that stuffy little case.'

'Yeah,' said George. 'And I bet the Prof's tied up in that long thin one. It's just his size.'

'What about the parcel?' asked Mophead.

'The shrinker. Right, kids – what do we do now?'

They didn't know. None of them. They looked at each other baffled. The two size spies walked jauntily towards a vast silver jet and disappeared up a long staircase into its main door. With shocking suddenness the engine noise, which they hadn't even noticed in the bustling airport, rose to a screaming roar that shook the balcony.

Then the plane started to turn and trundle towards its runway.

The spies were going to get away.

CHAPTER TWENTY

Chaos

It seemed like ages that they stood there. The plane glinted in the afternoon light as it turned. Like a monstrous, overgrown toy, it lumbered towards the observation platform. It was going to taxi right past them.

Cynthia let out a long, low wail of misery.

'Oh, oh, oh!' she said. 'We've got to stop it. Will somebody *do* something!'

Somebody did. With a sort of grunting bark the Snark launched himself towards the parapet. He leapt, stood for a second looking down at the ground yards and yards and yards below, then leapt again.

'Snark!' screamed George. 'You'll kill yourself!'

Dougal, not to be outdone, shot towards the parapet. But Jugears was too fast for him. He grabbed him by the collar and swung him back to safety as he was actually sailing over the top.

'You dopey dog,' he shouted. 'You're not electric!'

'Oh!' said Cynthia. 'He's hit! He's down!' she screeched. 'He's up again! He's all right! He's running for the plane!'

As one child and a dog they turned and burst into the observation lounge. If the Snark could do something, so could they, even if it wasn't jump to their certain deaths. They ran through the busy room scattering coffee tables and drinks like confetti. They didn't even have time to say sorry. People yelled and shouted, waiters tried to stop them. But on they raced, following the lead of the Snark.

It was a long way. They burst out of the lounge, along the corridor, to the steps. They were broad and crowded. Everyone gaped as the kids leapt them two at a time, darting in and out, avoiding porters carrying heavy suitcases. Dougal was barking madly and tripping people up right left and centre.

When they were almost down, two waiters and a policeman appeared at the top of the steps.

'Stop them!' they roared. 'They've smashed up the lounge! They must be thieves!'

Instantly the shout went up. 'Stop thief! Stop thief!' But the football strips came in useful now. Though dozens of hands reached out for them, there was little to grab. One woman was left holding the number nine from Mophead's shirt, and George lost a sleeve. But no one stopped them.

Dougal played his part well too. Although he was really a friendly, rather soft dog, he was very ginger and hairy. Leaping, barking and snapping his bright teeth he managed to make several people keep their distance.

And all the time Cynthia kept shouting: 'It's not us, you fools! It's not us! It's the spies! It's the size spies! They've nicked our ma and pa!'

'Oh shut up, Cynth,' George yelled. 'Save your breath to cool your porridge!'

In the big entrance hall they slipped and skidded on the polished floor. Jugears and Mophead, who had soccer boots on, were worst off. George and Cynthia had on plimsolls. They grabbed the boys' arms and pulled and pushed them along – leaving dreadful stud marks on the posh-looking floor.

'Where now?' said George. 'Jugears, which way do we go? Do you know?'

Jugears, sliding and slipping like a bad ice-skater, pointed towards a big double door.

'Through there. Baggage hall, then the Customs. We'll have to look sharp. It's crawling with guards and cops and that.'

By now there were a couple of dozen people running after them shouting. But the hall was so crowded that people in front, hearing the commotion, kept running the wrong way, and asking useless questions. Soon there was a great noisy confused jumble.

Suddenly a big man in uniform stepped out from behind a pillar. He loomed up in front of Mophead and put out his hand. He couldn't miss.

'Look out,' screeched Mophead, pointing past the man. 'Stop thief! There he goes! Stop thief!'

He was only tricked for a second, but it was enough. Mophead jinked, skidded, bounced off the pillar, and was away. Dougal gave the man's trouser leg a nice hard bite for good measure.

In the baggage hall the floor had matting down, so Jugears and Mophead could keep up. They ran through without any trouble, although the noise behind them was getting deafening.

Then it was the Customs ahead. A long room. Men in uniforms. Barriers. George gasped.

'Follow me,' Jugears hissed.

They went pounding on, almost with steam coming out of their ears. The Customs men, not knowing what was happening, stood like dummies. They watched the children and the dog. They watched the crowd stream in behind them. They listened to the shouting.

By the time it fully dawned what was going on, the kids were all heading straight for one of the small barriers. The Customs men nearly fell over each other in the struggle to block the way. Everyone seemed to be determined to make the arrest.

Within seconds the narrow passageway with the barrier was stuffed full of blue-uniformed officers. Jugears, Mophead, Cynthia, George and Dougal were only six feet away.

'Right,' yelled Jugears. 'Left!'

It was a daft enough order – Right, left! – but they knew

what he meant. Even Dougal switched direction like
magic. In an instant they'd crawled under the barrier and
through an unguarded passageway. The Customs men
were furious. They nearly blew their tops trying to catch
the kids. They didn't have a chance!

They burst out of the hall into the afternoon air. Dougal
spotted the Snark at once. He barked, running towards
him.

As the strange party sped across the airfield, the
observation balcony got fuller and fuller with goggling
people. The children spread out in a line over the runway
like refugees from some weird football team. Jugears,
panting and red, was even still clutching the ball. He was
first behind Dougal, then came Cynthia, then Mophead,
then George. The Snark was at the far side, standing in an
odd bent position, with one eye on them and the other
cocked at the aeroplane.

The aeroplane, the huge silver aeroplane, was pointing
directly at them. They formed a line right across its path.
And the aeroplane was picking up speed for its take-off.

'Stop,' George shouted.

The children stopped.

'Stand still,' said George. 'Just stand still. They won't
run us down.'

They stood. They gulped. Dougal started scratching for fleas. Pretending he doesn't care, thought Cynthia.

The noise from the aeroplane was becoming awful. It was whistling towards them fast now. They could hear the hissing of its mighty tyres on the tarmac. They all looked up in awe. A big jet plane is huge. Higher than a house, wider than a football pitch. George and Cynthia had never realised. They looked so tiny in the sky.

There were other noises too. Sirens, and screams, and the gunning of big diesel engines. From behind every building poured a horde of people and vehicles. Police cars, ambulances, fire tenders. There were men in army uniform clinging to an armoured car, dozens of police, fire-fighters in white flameproof suits looking like spacemen. They were spearing out towards the runway from every

point, determined to stop the crazy football team at all costs.

Blimey Moses, thought George. We've really started something this time.

The silver jet was very close indeed when it started to brake. It was so close, in fact, that it was much too late. The children trembled. Without them realising it the line closed up until they found themselves holding hands. The Snark, who was limping badly and leaking oil from a deep wound, snuggled up to Cynthia's leg. Dougal was in Mophead's arms.

The world was full of noise and horror. Over above them the vast snout of the aircraft towered, blotting out the sky. The great tyres, with the brakes full on, were gushing out thick black smoke and red flames as they screamed and tore across the tarmac. The roar of the engines, the rushing of wind – it was all too much. The children without a word, formed a ring with their dogs, held each other tight, and closed their eyes.

Waiting to be crushed by those monstrous, grinding, smoking, burning wheels. Waiting for the end.

CHAPTER TWENTY ONE

The Ultimate Weapon

The end didn't come. But in a way, what did happen was even worse. They stood there with their eyes tightly shut for what felt like an age. Until the smell of burning rubber made their throats ache. Until the heat glowing from the giant tyres made their skin hurt. Until the screeching, squealing, skidding din made their ears ring.

Then, with a thudding, creaking noise, louder even than the jet engines, the plane juddered to a halt.

Somehow, George knew. He opened his eyes. About a foot from them, black and smoking, much taller than any of the children, was a wheel. Two wheels, close together. Above them a huge leg disappearing into the vast silver wing.

'It's stopped!' he shouted. 'It's stopped! We've stopped it!'

The others opened their eyes. They were white and shaken. They began to cough from the filthy black smoke pouring off the tyres.

'We've stopped it!' coughed Cynthia. 'Oh, George, we've stopped it!'

They spread out into a line again, still holding hands. The Snark gave a warning bark.

All around them the children saw men. The horde that had raced from the airport buildings. In front, coming right up to them, was a big police officer in a flat cap with lots of silver on it. He looked very angry. Behind all the men, the soldiers, the firemen, the police, were the vehicles, grouped in a frightening half-circle.

The police officer was furious. As he reached them he
was shouting: 'What do you think you're doing? Have you
gone mad? Are you escaped lunatics? You could have
caused thousands of pounds worth of damage!'

Thanks very much, thought Cynthia! What about
us!

'We had to stop it!' yelled George. 'It's not our fault, it's
the Customs'. There are two spies on board. They've stolen
our mum and dad!'

'And the shrinker machine,' added Mophead. 'It's a
super thing.'

'You can get it back now,' said Jugears. 'You'll get a
medal. They might even make you a sergeant.'

As the officer was a chief superintendent this remark
didn't help.

'Spies!' he spluttered. 'Shrinker machines! You barmy
young toads, you'll never see the light of day again for
this!'

He made a sweep with his arm and ten or twelve burly
constables clomped past him.

'Come on,' they said. 'We'll 'ave to ask you down to the
station to answer some questions.'

'Get away!' said Cynthia. 'Get away or we'll set the dogs
on you!'

The policemen stopped, looking nervously over their
shoulders at the superintendent.

'We've got dogs too!' he snarled. 'We've got dogs that'll
make mincemeat of your dogs!'

He looked behind him and shouted: 'Dogs! Bring up the
dogs!'

The Snark and Dougal, who'd been looking their very
fiercest, wilted like dead daffodils when the police dogs
arrived. They were huge and horrible, with dripping
fangs. Alsatians that could have snapped up a normal
animal in two bites.

'Now will you come quietly?' said the superintendent.
'Or do we have to use force?'

'But please, please listen,' George pleaded. 'It's true. It's all true. If you move us the plane will go and we'll lose our parents!'

'And the Prof!' wailed Cynthia.

'And the shrinker!' shouted Jugears. 'It's a smashing thing, Mister! Much too good for a couple of silly spies!'

The superintendent merely smirked.

'All right, men,' he said. 'You know your duty. Arrest these dangerous criminals!'

The squad of policemen clomped forward. One put out his hand to Cynthia, who immediately bit it as hard as she possibly could.

'That'll be another five years!' he said nastily, and clipped her behind the ear.

The children fought hard, but they were no match for twelve policemen. The dogs, too, did their best. But Dougal was very little, and the poor Snark had been badly hurt in his leap from the balcony. It was all over in a couple of minutes.

When they were pulled clear the whine of the engines began to build up to a roar again. They stood in a helpless bunch, surrounded by blue uniforms, watching through their tears as the aeroplane built up power for take-off.

'I wish I were dead,' said Cynthia. 'Oh these silly grown-ups! I wish we'd been squashed. That would have stopped the rotten sly spies!'

The great silver machine was beginning to trundle slowly forward when the incredible happened. With a crash the escape hatch in its side flew open. And out of it poured the most amazing sound.

It was so loud that it all but drowned out the noise of the jets at full power. It was a mixture of what sounded like dozens of brass bands gone potty, along with two or three regiments of Scottish pipers who'd been let loose in a whisky warehouse. It was absolutely the most amazing and appalling sound the world had ever heard.

'Golly gumbos!' breathed George. 'It's our dad!'

As one body the policemen, the soldiers and the space-suited firemen dropped back several paces. They were flabbergasted. They were stunned. Two whole platoons of commandos dropped their rifles and put their fingers in their ears.

As everyone goggled the jet noise dropped from a roar to a whine again. The aircraft lumbered to a halt. And at the same time, the phenomenal music swelled louder and ever louder.

'Hail Smiling Morn!' gasped Cynthia.

'And Amazing Grace!' said George.

'And the Posthorn Gallop!' said Cynthia.

'And Under the Double Eagle! Hey listen, Cynth! He's even got the fluff in the Gallop.'

They were so relieved that they laughed aloud. Nobody else was laughing, though.

Least of all the spies. At that moment they came slipping and sliding into view, down the escape chute and into a heap on the ground. They took one terrified look around, picked up their peculiar-shaped luggage, and ran. From one of the cases, small and like a birdcage, with breathing holes in the sides, poured the massed music of all the military bands in England and Scotland.

'Hooray!' screamed George. 'He's panicked them! They're making a run for it! Come on, you lot! Up and at 'em!'

No one tried to stop the kids. They slipped out of the shocked fingers of the burly policemen easily. They'd gone well over a hundred yards before the grown-ups even began to pull themselves together.

When George realised they were alone, he stopped. He waved to the superintendent frantically.

'Come *on*!' he yelled. 'Don't you understand *anything*! They're spies! They'll get away!'

As he raced to catch up with the others, the super-intendent and the army officers scratched their heads and talked in low voices. They all agreed that something fishy was going on but they weren't sure what they ought to do. In the end it was the police dogs that made up their minds for them. Overcome by the excitement of seeing the Snark and Dougal galloping across the tarmac after the men with the noise, they strained and tugged at their leashes. First one, then two, then all of them, decided to go and join in. So that was that. The huge strong dogs were off! And their handlers had to go too – on their noses if they didn't use their legs to keep up.

The alsatians led, the dog handlers followed, the superintendent ran after them with his squad of clomping policemen. Slowly the armoured cars and the infantry and the fire tenders joined the chase.

Desperate men, the spies were. And Mrs Ponsonby-Smythe, who was pushing the Prof on his wheelie-suitcase and carrying the shrinker, was strong too. They kept up a cracking pace, even getting out of sight a couple of times. But Father's racket made sure they could never get out of earshot.

The children and their dogs followed the spies behind hangars, through fuel dumps, up and down flights of stairs. It was tiring work. Behind them came the others – horns blaring, sirens wailing, engines thundering. The business of the airport had come to a halt. Everyone was chasing the spies. Overhead great passenger plane pilots dodged each other in the sky and wondered why they could get no answer from flight control.

It ended very suddenly when the fat man and Mrs Ponsonby-Smythe ran round the corner of an engine-testing shed into a yard. In front of them was a twelve-foot brick wall. To their left was the shed. To the right was a hangar. They'd reached a dead end.

The children went as close as they dared, then stopped. The spies glared at them, their chests heaving, sweat pouring down their faces. The music from the small case was less regular now. Father was losing puff. In a short pause George shouted 'It's all right, Dad. You can shut up!' and the music started again, went on for a bar or two, faltered and stopped.

In the few seconds before the other people arrived the big, stubbly-chinned spy unwrapped the funny-looking parcel. By the time the army, the police and the fire-brigade had completely blocked off the only escape route, the shrinking machine, on its three spindly legs, was set up. It was pointing straight at them.

The police superintendent and a top army officer came over to the children.

'What is it?' they whispered.

George told them quickly. They seemed a bit afraid.

'Hhm,' said the superintendent at last. 'Looks like a job for the Government. How long will they be?'

The army officer looked at his watch.

'I radioed about ten minutes ago,' he said. 'If they come by helicopter it won't be long. Let's get some armoured cars and tanks up to point at these chaps, eh? No need to rush 'em just yet.'

The two spies were getting their breath back. Mrs Ponsonby-Smythe was fiddling busily with the machine.

'But you've got to!' said Cynthia. 'He won't have been able to get it ready to fire yet. It takes quite a time!'

'If you rush them now,' added George, 'you'll be all right. But if you wait I can't think what might happen!'

'Nonsense!' said the army officer. 'We know best, kiddies!'

'Yes,' said the superintendent. 'Leave it to your elders and betters.'

And that, for the moment, was that.

CHAPTER TWENTY TWO

An Error of Judgement

It wasn't many minutes, in fact, before the Government arrived. They came in a big, highly-polished helicopter, and they did not come alone. There were butlers, footmen, valets, and a special tea-maker. Another serving man, dressed in a plum-coloured tail-coat, carried a small fat barrel with a silver handle, a bunch of bananas, and several packets of nuts. Although the children did not know it at the time, he was the official between-meals-snacks-specialist. In the barrel there were seven sorts of biscuits, many of them chocolate.

The Government, flanked by their servants and surrounded by the men in mackintoshes with bulges under their arms, pushed their way to the front of the crowd. Mr Grandison Splatt, Mrs Sylvester Savoy and Doberman Dooley eyed up the situation curiously. At last Mr Splatt spoke to the superintendent and the army chief.

'Well, now,' he said. 'What's going on here, then? Fine how d'ye do, pulling us out of a Cabinet meeting like that. We've got a country to run, you know.'

'Yes indeed,' added Mrs Sylvester Savoy, pulling her fur wrap closer around her shoulders. 'Quite chilly, isn't it?'

'For the time of year,' said Doberman Dooley with a smile. 'Care for a cup of tea?'

As if by magic the man in charge of the tea came forward with his trolley. The Government took their cups and turned to the biscuit-keeper. There was a hush in the vast crowd as they sipped and munched. Mr Grandison Splatt, to Cynthia's amazement, dunked his gingernut into his cup. (George didn't care either way.)

The army chief coughed in a nervous fashion.

'Ahem,' he said. 'I don't wish to rush matters, your worshipfuls, but we do have rather a tight situation here.'

Mr Splatt turned a sour gaze on him.

'Shut up,' he said. 'Can't you see we're having a nice cup of tea?'

'Clears the brain,' added Mrs Sylvester.

'Anyway, can't do anything till the others get here, now can we?' said Doberman Dooley.

Mr Splatt was the Prime Minister. It appeared that no one could speak until he did, then the others always said something in turn, even if there was nothing to be said.

Cynthia and George, watching the spies while all this was going on, saw Mrs Ponsonby-Smythe stand upright with a big, triumphant grin.

'Oh cripes, George,' said Cynthia. 'He's ready. Oh gosh, now what'll happen?'

For the moment, nothing. Then Mr Grandison Splatt, handing back his cup, asked to be told what was the trouble. Mrs Sylvester Savoy and Doberman Dooley added their bits of nonsense. The police superintendent and the army chief told them of the chase and all three tut-tutted at the naughty behaviour of the children.

'But what exactly is this machine meant to do?' said Splatt.

'Why don't you just sort of . . . take it off them?' added Mrs Sylvester.

'I say, any more custard creams?' said Doberman Dooley.

When they heard what the machine was meant to do, they got very heated. The Minister of Extremely Secret Things, who'd been hovering in the background, was called forward to explain. He insisted he'd told them all about it, they insisted that he hadn't. When they asked him what ought to be done, he didn't hesitate.

'Charge,' he said firmly. 'The whole thing is utterly ridiculous. I mean no one could *really* believe it, could they? A shrinking machine? Impossible!'

'It's *not* impossible,' Cynthia snapped. 'You're the one that's impossible! It's all your silly fault!'

The Government all yawned noisily. Children, children, they seemed to be saying. What rubbish they talk!

'Well we can't charge yet,' said Mr Grandison Splatt. 'Out of the question.'

'They're not here, you see,' said Mrs Sylvester Savoy.

'Hold on, though,' added Dooley. 'I do believe they've arrived.'

There was a murmuring and clattering of boots among the massed ranks of soldiers and policemen. A strange procession came into view. With shouts of 'Make way there' and 'Clear a path', seventeen TV camera crews, one hundred and forty seven Gentlemen of the Press, seven hundred various helpers, and three thousand two hundred and eleven Civil Servants pushed into the space between the buildings. There was a flurry of flashbulbs and the

rustling of a myriad notebooks as the Government posed for pictures and gave interviews.

The children were in despair. They just couldn't believe this could be happening. They didn't know what to do.

Oddly, it was the spies who broke up the party. They too had got bored. They too must have decided the Government were going too far. In the midst of the posing and TV, Mr Fixit let out a yell.

'Hoi!' he shouted. 'Vot is all thees nonsense, heh? Ve are in ze hurry. Kindly get on wiz it!'

The Government were disgusted. But the fattest man in the world was not going to be ignored.

'Ve gives you five seconds from now! If you don't get us out of heres, viz a plane to fly us home double quicker, we shrinks you all to ze sizing from ze chocolate mouses!'

Mrs Ponsonby-Smythe gave one of his horrible laughs.

'Zen maybe ve are eating you all up, heh? Zat vould be nice.'

Mr Grandison Splatt, Mrs Sylvester Savoy and Doberman Dooley had gone pale at these threats. They backed off a bit, calling on the Secrets Minister to advise. He flapped his hands about and looked very clever.

'Nonsense,' he cried. 'It's all nonsense! Call their bluff!'

Cynthia opened her mouth to speak. George stopped her.

'Don't waste your breath, Cynth,' he whispered. 'Just get ready to run for it.'

The Prime Minister looked sternly at the spies.

'Now listen, lads,' he shouted. 'Don't be silly. We've got you trapped. And don't let's hear any more of this shrinking rubbish.'

'You see, we don't believe in that sort of thing,' shrilled the lady.

'Because we're British,' added Doberman Dooley. 'Yes.'

The two spies looked at each other. They whispered together. Then the fat man abruptly opened the wheelie-suitcase and the Prof sat up, looking sick and tired.

'You morons,' he shouted. 'For the sake of sanity listen to what these chaps are talking about. It's no joke, you know. This machine actually *works*.'

The Minister of Extremely Secret Things gave a snort of disgust.

'Of course it does,' he yelled back. 'Just like the Monkey Machine!'

The Government roared with laughter. So did the superintendent and the army boss. The Prof sank back into his case and pulled the lid down again. He couldn't bear to look at them.

'Vell?' said Fixit. 'Do ve get ze plane?'

'Never!' said Grandison Splatt.

'Not at all,' said Mrs S.S.

'Think we'd listen to that old twit?' said Dooley.

The fat man did a little dance of fury. He whispered something to his big, blue-chinned assistant. Mrs Ponsonby-Smythe picked up the small case with breathing holes. He undid the clips, pulled off the top, put down the box and pulled out two tiny figures.

George and Cynthia would have loved to have shouted comforting words. But they had a horrible feeling that now the Government were in charge something terrible was bound to happen. They kept quiet.

'*Now* will you belief us?' asked Mr Fixit. 'Zere are ze leedle people. Zat is how you vill be if you are not double quicker!'

The big spy added: 'Like ze chockie mouses, remember? To be munched and crunched!'

To be fair, the Government actually looked shaken by this. The army chief stared through his binoculars and said that they appeared to be real people, only very, very tiny. But the Secrets Minister just laughed louder.

'A trick!' he said. 'It's a trick! If you let yourselves be taken in by a thing like that you'll be a laughing stock!'

They still didn't look sure. The parents seemed very lifelike, even at that distance.

'You'll lose votes,' he shouted. 'People will say you're too silly. Much too silly. And they won't vote for you.'

The Government went into a huddle. The children, who could hear a lot of what they said, thought they were very anxious to all appear braver than each other. They somehow talked themselves into a situation they couldn't get out of without seeming soppy. Just like kids, thought Cynthia. Just how wars start thought George, who'd read a lot of history.

After a couple of minutes, Fixit shouted again.

'Zis time I mean eet,' he said. 'I am counting up to five, zen my friend is pressing ze button. You haf been warned.'

But he only got up to two.

Then Mr Grandison Splatt, Mrs Sylvester Savoy, and Doberman Dooley, turned to the superintendent of police and the high-ranking army officer. All together they said: 'Charge.'

The order was given in a flash. And as the troops began to move in, Mrs Ponsonby-Smythe, with a horrible grin, pressed the button.

CHAPTER TWENTY THREE

Before Your Very Eyes

Without being told to, all the policemen and soldiers stopped. They stared about them in a worried fashion. The Government too, and all their helpers, seemed at a loss. In fact the only people to move were the children. Cynthia grabbed Mophead and Dougal and raced out of the line of the shrinker machine. George had to pick up the injured Snark, then he pushed Jugears towards the others. They pressed themselves against the brick wall.

'Cross your fingers!' said Cynthia. It was daft, but they all did.

At first, nothing at all happened. There was an eerie silence over everything, with only the quiet grumbling of engines in the background. At one end of the yard stood the size spies, tense and waiting, at the other the Government and their troops, anxious and still. The Prof lay in his box behind the spies, and the parents' box was behind the Prof's.

After what seemed like ages, although it can only have been a few seconds, a strange whining noise made itself heard. It was a cross between a buzz and a hum, rather like bees on a hot summer's day. It got quite loud. Still no one moved.

'That's the machine,' Cynthia whispered to Jugears and Mophead. 'That's the noise it made before the parents had their accident.'

'It won't be long now I don't think,' George added. 'Oh dear I wonder what'll happen.'

Mophead poked Jugears in the ribs.

'I hope you get shrunk,' he said. 'Then I'll be able to bash you up for all the times you've done it to me!'

The noise rose. Everyone was still, like statues. In the background the television cameras whirred softly.

Then, slowly, very slowly, the thing began to happen. It was Cynthia who spotted it.

'Look!' she shouted. 'Oh look! He's getting smaller! Mrs Ponsonby-Smythe!'

A gasp went up from the crowd. It was true. You could hardly tell it at first, but the big, unshaven, hairy ex-charperson and part-time spy was getting smaller. Already he was down to five foot eleven, and he was starting to dwindle faster.

The spy let out a shriek.

'Vot is happenink to me?' he shouted. 'I am feeling down in ze mouth. Help! Help! Everyzink she is gettink bigger!'

He was only five foot three by the time he'd said all that. He grabbed a handful of crew-cut and tried to pull himself taller again. Mr Fixit shook his head sadly as his friend shortened.

'Ach my leedle pal,' he said. 'Don't leave me like zis! Stay as beeg as you were! Who is going to be carryink ze luggage?'

'You fool!' screeched Ponsonby-Smythe. 'Zis is all your faulty! You got me into zis mess! You it voz who says to pressing ze button. You said ze Professor knew his carrots!'

Fixit shook his head.

'Onions, my boy, onions,' he said. 'I said he vos knowing his onions.'

'Votever he is knowing he voz knowing wronk!' squeaked Ponsonby-Smythe. Squeaked is the word. His voice was getting high and thin by the second.

Mophead nudged George.

'Hey, look,' he said. 'Now old Fatso's going!'

He was. There was another gasp of wonder from the crowd. 'Old Fatso' was losing weight. And fast.

It turned into a race. Mrs Ponsonby-Smythe was getting

shorter in leaps and bounds, while Mr Fixit was shedding pounds and pounds as though he was being melted. He went from about twenty-two stone down to fifteen stone six (or thereabouts) in two minutes flat.

'Oh, oh, oh, oh, oh!' he roared. The first 'oh' was in his normal voice, the fifth in someone else's altogether. A thinner person's, a lighter person's. A smaller person's.

In a few more seconds it was all over bar the shouting. The two spies *shot* towards the ground for the last few feet. One disappeared down one side of the shrinker, the other down the other. They stopped, with a jerk, when the big one was seven inches high and the little one was four and a half in his socks.

There was a pause, broken only by a sound like the mewing of new-born kittens. The spies were having a good old cry.

Then the shouting started. And what a commotion everyone set up! There was cheering, and yelling, and applause. Cries of 'Speech!' to the Government, cries of 'Clear a path!' from the television crews.

Within moments everyone had forgotten everything except the triumphant victory over the nasty spies. Floodlights were brought forward, make-up girls dabbed powder on the shiny faces of Mr Grandison Splatt, Mrs Sylvester Savoy and Doberman Dooley. The cameras began to roll once more, while flashbulbs popped from the dozens and dozens of men from the newspapers.

'Yes,' said Splatt. 'I think I can safely say that as Prime Minister, I've saved the nation from one of the worst disasters in the history of the universe.'

'With the help, of course,' put in Mrs Sylvester Savoy, 'of myself. It was I who advised—'

Doberman Dooley interrupted: 'Yes yes, good lady, but you must agree that it was *me* . . . '

The children didn't wait to hear more. They'd been forgotten, too, of course, as had the parents, the Prof, the spies and the machine. They sidled along the wall, keeping well out of its beam, and George and Cynthia crawled the last few yards on their stomachs, like Indian scouts. The two brothers and the dogs had other business to attend to. They went off, with Jugears still clutching his football.

The shrinker was humming and buzzing loudly. It was also beginning to glow red. George stuck out a careful finger and pressed the 'Stop' button. With a noise like a sigh, the machine slowly went dead.

He gave a whistle of relief.

'Phew. I'm glad that's over. Blimey, though, aren't those Government people the giddy—'

'Shut up, George,' hissed Cynthia. 'Listen!'

The babble of voices, and cheers, and happy chatter from the other end of the yard was changing. There was a scream. Then a series of yells. Then there was the clattering of many feet. The crowd was scattering, running wildly.

'What's up?' said George. 'What's got into that lot?'

It wasn't long before the only people left in the ring of cameras and arc-lights were the Government and the television crews. Everyone else had pulled back twenty feet. They stood in a half circle with their eyes sticking out like organ stops.

And slowly, ever so ever so slowly, watched by the army, the police force, the fire brigade, and the world's Press and TV, the British Government shrank.

They didn't go quietly and they didn't go fast. In fact they threatened and promised and roared. They blustered, they blamed, they even swore. As their voices got squeakier, they were more certain than ever, so they said, that it was all a plot, and that someone had to save them.

'It shouldn't happen to a dog,' was the last thing anyone heard properly. 'Let alone to Her Majesty's Government!'

When they were the size of three wooden clothes pegs they stopped shrinking. The plum-coated servant, with great presence of mind, threw away the last of the gingernuts and popped them into the biscuit barrel.

CHAPTER TWENTY FOUR

The End of the Story

If it hadn't been for Jugears and Mophead, helped by Dougal and the Snark, the spies would have got clean away. George and Cynthia, after switching off the machine and watching the dwindling of the Government, were much too busy having a happy reunion with the parents and the Prof to care. At the other end of the yard, all was chaos. Soldiers were running about in panic, policemen were scratching their heads, Civil Servants were writing memos to each other. Nothing sensible was being done at all.

Jugears and Mophead had seen the tiny spies slipping along the opposite wall while the Government had been boasting to the cameras. The dogs soon picked up the scent and they bowled along happily, although the Snark, being badly bent, couldn't keep up too well.

At last they saw the tiny men in the middle of one of the runways. They were heading back towards their plane, which had stopped in all the excitement of course. The gangway had been put back up against it and they obviously planned to go on board and hide until it finally took off and carried them home.

'Run, run,' shouted Mophead. 'If they reach it before we do we'll never find them.'

They all put on their best speed, but it was too far. After a couple of minutes it looked certain that the spies would get away.

Suddenly Jugears stopped.

'Who's the best kicker in the school?' he asked.

Mophead didn't like to admit it, but he forced himself. 'You are,' he said.

Jugears dropped the football in front of him, trapped it, placed it carefully . . .

And WHAM!

It flew through the air in a high curve. The four and a half inch high fat man, three feet behind what was left of Mrs Ponsonby-Smythe, caught it square in the middle of the back. Over he went, rolling and squeaking.

By the time his faithful assistant had come back, picked him up, and dusted him off, the dogs were guarding the steps up to the plane. Two ticks later Mophead picked up the fat one and Jugears the thin. He also picked up the ball – and kissed it.

'Great shooting,' said Mophead. Then he added sourly: 'Big head!'

Of course, now that the Government had met with an unfortunate accident, too, there was no shortage of money for the Prof to carry on his experiments. In fact, life on the Yorkshire Moors got pretty luxurious. The roof was mended, the window frames were renewed, and there was never any shortage of food. The Prof was kept with a constant supply of funds and many friendly letters enquiring how the work was going on. He was to perfect the shrinking machine, because everyone realised now what a spiffing weapon it would be in a war, but he also had to get the deshrinker part of it working – in double quick time.

The size spies, strangely enough, came to the house on the moors too, They were installed in a well-fortified, specially-built prison house in a disused room near the living quarters at first, and they were to be used in the Prof's experiments on the deshrinker. But after a while Father started to visit them, mainly to play chess, and it wasn't long before they became friends. Mother invited them to be their guests in the doll's house, and she very

soon got back to being her jolly old self again. She revelled
in delighting them with her brilliant meals and cakes, and
the four of them had dinner parties nearly every night.

Long before the Prof had finished his work the spies had
become great favourites. They got passionately fond of
brass band music too. Father's one-man twenty-six piece
device – played much quieter now he was happy again –
was brought to a pitch of perfection. The exciting strains of
the Overture from Egmont, the happy brassiness of Seventy
Six Trombones, spread sweetly through the deserted
corridors. Cynthia and George even used to go and listen
for pleasure!

Everyone else in the house was happy too. The Snark was
stripped down and given a complete overhaul, so that after
he'd got over the shock of being switched on again he was
as good as new, Viva the unreliable cat got a new fuse and a
clean-up, and the Thinks Computer was practically rebuilt
from scratch. To the Prof's surprise, after all his efforts, it
still thought in verse. But it did tend to be better-tempered.

Finally, to the great joy of George and Cynthia, the
punishments book was chucked out. Father sent them a
message to visit him one day, and simply told them he'd
been silly.

'You've done a great job, kids,' he said with a smile. 'I
don't know how things would have been without you. You
must forgive your mother and me for being so bad-
tempered. It was the strain.'

'If we ever get back to normal,' Mum added. 'Far from
stopping you eating ice-cream, we'll give you as much as
you like. You can eat it till you're sick. All right?'

'All right except for one thing,' said George. 'It's not *if*
you get back to normal—'

'It's *when*,' said Cynthia.

When the Prof was ready to try out the deshrinker, the
ex-spies insisted that they should take the risk. The Prof
wasn't willing to experiment on anyone, but they absolutely forced his hand. It was all their fault, they said

(although of course it wasn't!) and they must face the consequences.

The deshrinking, which took place on the moor near the site of the original accident, was not a complete success. The men did become full-size again, but with one strange effect. The one who'd been tall and strong and lean became short and smallish and neat, and Mr Fixit, who'd been like a little fat barrel, shot up to nearly six feet, although he didn't get any thinner.

But they didn't mind at all. They'd picked up good local accents under Father's teaching and the Prof had no intention of turning them over to the police as he should have done. They changed their names to Gibson and Weston and went to help run a nearby brass band. And very well they did, too. The Prof merely reported that they'd escaped and that as they were still tiny there wasn't much point in searching for them.

It took him two more months to sort out why the ex-spies had been mixed up in the deshrinking, then he got in touch with the Government and told them he was ready. He suggested a quiet occasion, with no one else present. But they wouldn't hear of it.

In fact, when the great day came, it was like a coronation. A vast hall had been built specially, the press and television from all over the world were there, and tickets were on sale at up to fifty pounds a time, black-market.

The children, along with Jugears and Mophead, Cedric and Mabel and the two dogs, were in a special box out front, and leading off from it was the platform where the Prof stood with the shrinker/deshrinker. About twenty feet away was another platform, where the little people were to be placed.

The wait seemed like ages. There were speeches, and more speeches, and congratulations, and handshakings galore. The Prof, very uncomfortable in a morning suit with long tails and a white, tight tie, got more and more hot and bothered. When the children could see he was very near the end of his tether, there was a fanfare of trumpets. They were off.

A man in uniform brought a gilded box onto the other platform. One by one, to cheers and clapping, the little people stepped out. Mr Grandison Splatt, Mrs Sylvester Savoy, Doberman Dooley . . . and the parents.

After only one more speech – and quite a short one – the Prof was asked to begin. A hush fell on the great hall. You could have heard a pin drop. With a small bow, he pressed the button.

This time nothing at all went wrong. It worked like a dream. There was a low buzzing, a sigh of amazement from thousands of throats, then an absolute tumult of cheering.

There on the platform, smiling fit to bust, stood five full-size human beings. Just like that. Like magic.

The parents, and the Prof, and Cynthia and George, had hardly had time to race together to a storm of hugs, kisses and tears before the speeches started.

'Her Majesty's Government,' said Mr Grandison Splatt, 'have realised from the very start the incredible importance of this wonderful machine.'

'With it,' said Mrs Sylvester Savoy, 'we will bring peace to the world.'

'No army will be able to face us,' added Doberman Dooley. 'No navy can put to sea.'

'From this day forward,' said Mr Grandison Splatt, 'we are the conque . . .'

There was a blinding blue flash, a tremendous bang, and a column of fire from the platform where the machine had stood.

'Yes,' muttered the Prof. 'Well, I think we'd better be going, what my dears?'

In the chaos and confusion they all slipped out. Cedric drove them to the station, where everyone said fond goodbyes and arranged to meet for a holiday soon. Then they were on the train – first class! – and heading for home.

When they'd seen enough scenery and drunk enough pop and chatted to the parents about being big again, Cynthia and George woke up the Prof.

'Does that mean there'll be no more shrinker?' asked George. 'Can you rebuild it?'

The Prof smiled.

'I'm afraid not,' he said. 'You know I don't keep plans.'

'But why did you do it?' asked Cynthia. 'You did do it, didn't you? It wasn't an accident?'

He went on smiling.

'No, it wasn't an accident.'

'Go on, then,' said George.

'Well it was you two, really,' the Prof started. 'Always getting at me about scientists. How we tend to do things without thinking enough about what might happen. I finally came to the conclusion you were probably right.'

'Course we're right,' said Cynthia.

'Then again it was the Government. When I met them I had a lot more doubts, I must say. So . . . I asked the Thinks Computer.'

'And?' said George.

'Oh,' the Prof chuckled. 'It was very silly as usual. But right, I think.'

'What did it say?' asked Cynthia.

The Prof handed over a scrap of paper from his pocket. George and Cynthia read it together. This is what it said:

> The shrinker's a beautiful weapon
> But weapons aren't made to bring peace.
> So build in a stick
> Of dynamite quick
> If it's war they want – BANG – cook their geese.

'I don't get it,' said Cynthia. 'Why did it blow up?'
'Nobody mentioned war at all,' George added.

The Prof laughed out loud.

'No more they did, my dears,' he said. 'But peace was the key word. As soon as that was mentioned the shrinking machine had ten seconds left on earth. They brought it on themselves.'

Cynthia and George shook their heads.

'Nuts,' said Cynthia, and tapped her head with a finger.

'Cynthia,' said George. 'I'm afraid you're right.'

Albeson and the Germans

JAN NEEDLE

It seems a very simple thing that starts off all the trouble – a rumour that two German children are coming to Church Street School. Although the teachers cannot understand the panic that this causes, Albeson can. His comics, and his dead grandfather have taught him all about Germans. And he doesn't fancy the idea one little bit.

The plan that Albeson's friend Pam comes up with frightens him stiff. Unfortunately, his mate Smithie, who's very tough and sometimes a bit odd, likes the idea. So Albeson has no choice. From then on, everything Albeson does gets him deeper and deeper into trouble, and finally, danger.

'Gripping, lively and funny – It really grabs you'

Daily Mirror

Harriet the Spy

Louise Fitzhugh

Harriet the Spy has a secret notebook, which she fills with utterly honest jottings about her parents, her friends and her neighbours. This, she feels sure, will prepare her for her career as a famous writer. Every day on her spy route, she scrutinizes, observes and notes down anything of interest to her:

> Laura Peters is thinner and uglier. I think she could do with some braces on her teeth.

> Once I thought I wanted to be Franca. But she's so dull, if I was her I couldn't stand myself, I guess it's not money that makes people dull. I better find out because I might be it.

> If Marion Hawthorne doesn't watch out she's going to grow up into a lady Hitler.

But Harriet commits the unforgivable for a spy – she is unmasked. When her notebook is found by her school friends, their anger and retaliation and Harriet's unexpected responses explode in an hilarious and often touching way.

'Harriet M. Welsch is one of the meatiest heroines in modern juvenile literature. This novel is a *tour de force*.'

Library Journal

The Third Class Genie

ROBERT LEESON

Disasters were leading two nil on Alec's disaster-triumph scorecard, when he slipped into the vacant factory lot, locally known as the Tank. Ginger Wallace was hot on his heels, ready to destroy him, and Alec had escaped just in the nick of time. There were disasters awaiting him at home too, when he discovered that he would have to move out of his room and into the boxroom. And, of course, there was school . . .

But Alec's luck changed when he found a beer can that was still sealed, but obviously empty. Stranger still, when he held it up to his ear, he could hear a faint snoring . . . When Alec finally opened the mysterious can, something happened that gave triumphs a roaring and most unexpected lead.

A hilarious story for readers of ten upwards.

Harold and Bella, Jammy and Me

ROBERT LEESON

Our gang, Harold and Bella, Jammy and me, was always getting into some scrape or other. Playing Hallowe'en tricks on the Tunnel Top gang . . . Coming home soaked after we'd found the bridge over the stream up in the woods, and the other lot happened to come along . . . Investigating the caves where we'd heard King Arthur and his knights still slept . . .

Brimful of colourful characters and adventures, this is a lively and funny collection of stories about a group of children growing up in a Northern town.

Some other Fontana Lions by Robert Leeson are *Challenge in the Dark, The Demon Bike Rider, The Third Class Genie, Grange Hill Rules, O.K?, Grange Hill Goes Wild, Grange Hill For Sale* and *It's My Life.*